For those who want to live
a life worth remembering

O LITTLE TOWN OF BETHANY

Cover Photo Model: © Halfpoint - Fotolia.com
Snow Photo: © Christopher Price / Roads & Rivers Media
Interior Chapter Graphics Holly: © natasha_55 - Fotolia.com

Cover Design by: Christopher Price / Roads & Rivers Media

Purple PenWorks® is a registered trademark of Cheryl McKay, designed by Heather Gebbia.

Published in the United States of America

ISBN-13: 978-1-946344-01-4
ISBN-10: 1-946344-01-X

Second Edition 2018
Originally Published 2015 by Redbud Press / Serenade Books

DIVINE ROMANCE COLLECTION

O Little Town of Bethany

a Christmas novella

rene gutteridge
cheryl mckay

By Rene Gutteridge & Cheryl McKay

Never the Bride: a novel
Love's a Stage: a novel
O Little Town of Bethany: a novella
Greetings from the Flipside: a novel
Novelizations: How to Adapt Scripts Into Novels

The Ultimate Gift: feature film (by Cheryl McKay)
The Ultimate Gift: novelization (by Rene Gutteridge)

TABLE OF CONTENTS

Chapter One

This suffocating, starved-for-personality city.

Smog, normally high against the skyline, sank today, pushing against the metropolis, daring it to stay in place. The wind, brisk and biting, like its people, whipped against the Christmas bows tied to the solar-powered street lamps. Thanksgiving had not yet made it to the calendar, but here, in the city, Christmas was a commodity, not a holiday.

In the sea of people, the fast-forwards of the world, Holly Truesdale tried to stroll. She had to keep her eyes up. She'd never developed the skill of weaving around others without actually looking at them. Beside her a man juggled a cell phone between his cheek and his shoulder, using his hands to dig in his briefcase. In front of her, she marveled at a woman in five-inch heels, keeping pace, steady as a racehorse.

Somewhere along the way, she was sure Christmas music was being piped into the air, but nobody could hear it because of the honking. The honking, more than anything, rattled her nerves, even though she was practically born on the street — in a jewelry store two blocks over when her mom decided she *needed* to buy a diamond bracelet.

Holly finally made it to her office building. Stuffed into the elevator like a pimento in an olive, she stood with her shoulders folded forward and waited for the fifth floor. Someone had eaten an everything bagel this morning.

Once the doors slid open and she slid out, she greeted Abigail, but Abigail did not greet her.

"Control X Security, please hold. Control X Security, please hold. Control X Security, how may I direct your call?"

Holly waited, because deep in her heart, she felt that life was about people, and people needed to connect, and saying hello to someone in the morning was important.

Abigail continued to navigate early morning phone calls at the receptionist's desk, so Holly stared at the huge display of glass shelves that showcased the progression of information deleting: multi-cut scissors, the antique pasta shredder which inspired old school shredders, samples of straight cut, cross-cuts, and then on through modern computer deletion devices and CD shredders, all neatly labeled with dates of invention.

Abigail took a breath. Holly pounced. "Good morning, Abigail!"

Abigail tried a friendly wave, but it looked more like the last hand to go underwater before a drowning.

Holly continued on to her office.

If the outside streets were suffocating, the inside of her building at Control X Security was like a buzzing fluorescent light. She went to her office, the one that said "manager" on the door placard, and pulled up the blinds, letting the dismal day's light in. No matter how gloomy it was, she always preferred natural light over artificial.

She shut the office door and locked it, though nobody would come in without knocking.

Placing her hands behind her back, she looked out the window and said, "Noah...we're just...you and I are two different...people. I mean, you feel that too, don't you, Noah?"

Her faint reflection stared back at her in the window.

"Yep. You got this."

After unlocking her office door, she marched down the first hallway, turned right, turned left, and intended to take another left when she ran into a hulk of a man, otherwise known as her father.

"Daddy! Sorry about that, I..." She smiled slightly. "Excuse me. I mean Mr. Truesdale." He insisted on the formal name during work hours. *As owner of the company*, he would say before explicit instructions to her, whatever those instructions might be. As if she could forget. He reminded her every day, without even saying it.

His nose was in a folder. "Hello, Holliston."

They rarely had much to say to each other, but she stroked the leaf of a fake tree next to them and gave it a try. "This needs a strand of Christmas lights, don't you think?"

"If you say so. Don't forget, staff meeting tomorrow at eleven. We have a lot of work coming up for the end of year shreds. Some of our biggest corporate clients are ready to forget the less noteworthy parts of their year. Don't make big Christmas plans." He continued down the hall. "Would you tell that mother of yours that her allowance for the month is already blown?"

"Why don't you tell her yourself?" Holly grabbed onto the fake branch to give her hands something to do. Why did she still feel like a kid when she talked back to him?

"She won't throw a plate at you."

And he was gone around the corner.

She continued on her path and made it to Noah's office. His placard was bigger. She stared at his name: NOAH DAY, V.P. Holly Day always sounded nice to her, but she knew hoping to marry into a nice last name was not enough to hold a relationship together. Her friend, Isabelle, had once married a Gerald Hupperskiwitz. They lived happily ever after, even though Isabelle could barely pronounce her own name and loathed the amount of time it took to get her signature on paper.

She went into Noah's office. He did a little wave, the one he always did when he couldn't manage to tear his eyes off his monitor. His back was toward her, his nose was four inches from the screen. She observed him, thinking through the list she'd made when they began to date. He was responsible, secure, and not bad looking. She'd yet to fill out the other two of her top five things she appreciated about him.

And that was why she was here. Perhaps it was more appropriate to do it out of the office, but they hardly saw each other anywhere else.

Clearly, though, this wasn't a good time. She slumped, leaning on his desk with her palms flat against the wood. "Hey, uh, Noah?"

"Hmm?"

"Would you...could we...do you have any time later? Tonight maybe?"

"Later."

"That's what I said."

Suddenly he swung his arm backward, the way someone would do to loosen a muscle, but then he pointed to a small black box sitting near the edge of his desk.

"That finally came. I was supposed to give it to you last weekend when we had that nice lunch."

"Early Christmas? What is it?"

She picked it up and popped it open. He always thought she liked jewelry because her mom liked jewelry. He never seemed to notice she didn't even wear earrings. She stretched a smile across her mouth, mimicking her mother's reaction to any kind of jewel, preparing herself for a bracelet she would never like but would have to wear.

But it was not a bracelet, or earrings, or necklace.

It was, of all things, an engagement ring. She choked on nothing but air.

"Uh...Noah?"

"Pretty, huh? I had Belvedere, your mom's guy, help me pick it out. Tasteful but big, right? Listen, I can't talk now," he said, his finger tracing some spreadsheet line on his computer. "I'm on a rush scrub for Heritage Trust and..."

He had this habit of letting his words trail off, like he forgot he was speaking, like whatever was on his mind was more important.

He didn't notice when she set the box back on his desk and slipped out.

Chapter Two

Behind her parents' mansion, all 5,912 square feet of it, stood a quaint guest house which suited Holly just fine. She insisted she pay rent for it, though she could easily afford a small apartment in the city. But she didn't want a city life. Suburbia wasn't quite right either, but at least the air was cleaner. Paying for rent, she supposed, was a small way that she could control her life. Everything else seemed planned for her. She was due to receive a large inheritance and trust fund at the age of 35, none of which she wanted. The more that was given to her, the more control her family wanted. So she paid rent, gave the majority of her overblown paycheck to charity, and put the last little bit in savings. What she was saving for was anyone's guess. What she really wanted was to make her own way.

The sun had already set by the time she headed for the living room and plopped into the comfy wingback, the one her mom was going to toss to the curb. She watched Carmen, her parents' housecleaner, dust methodically and quickly.

"I'm sorry I'm a little behind today, Holly. Let's just say the Roomba Vacuum had an appetite for your mother's custom designed lace curtains."

"The French ones?" Holly couldn't help the ornery smile.

"Yes, those," Carmen said. Where Holly's mother spent endless dollars trying to keep her appearance young, Carmen, well into her sixties, looked at least a decade younger than she was. Perhaps it was her glowing, tanned skin, but Holly thought a good dose of happiness in her life was probably what kept her youthful.

"I'm sure she took that well."

"Oh, you know your mother. She loves to exercise those vocal cords."

"And bench press her credit limit. I really wish you wouldn't clean for me."

"But then who would I have to talk to?" She lifted a lamp and winked as she glided the duster around on the table.

"You have any special Christmas plans, Carmen?"

"My son is coming in with his wife and my new grandbaby, Sharon. It'll be a tight squeeze at the house, but I just want to savor every minute, you know?"

Holly sunk deeper into her chair, glancing

around at any sign that she did, in fact, know what Carmen meant.

"I got one of those...what do you call them? Digital cameras? So I can take thousands of pictures. I'm going to drive them nuts!" Carmen waved her feather duster in the air. "How was work today, dear Holly?"

"You mean other than the most unmemorable marriage proposal of every girl's dreams?"

"Oh dear..." Carmen dropped her duster to the table and rushed to Holly's side. She perched on the coffee table in front of her. "Tell me."

"Is it still a proposal if the man never technically asks?"

"I don't even know what that means but..." She grabbed Holly's hand, inspected her empty ring finger. "Oh, thank goodness. I mean...I'm sorry. I shouldn't—"

"Carmen," Holly said, "you know I can't talk to my mother. She has more than enough ideas for my life. What do you think? I want to know...off the family record."

Holly watched Carmen's face. As hard as her parents were to work for, Carmen was lovely to them, loyal, and had worked for them almost as long as Holly had been alive.

"I think, well, I'd like to know what you think. What you want."

"That matters?" Holly looked at an empty wall,

a wall where pictures would normally hang, in a normal-type house.

"It should." Carmen nodded, her face solemn. "To you. You remember when you were five, maybe six, and we watched those little bluebirds in the back yard? Nesting. Hatching. And then you thought the momma bird, that she was being cruel when it came time to push them out."

"They could barely fly."

"But they did. In case no one's ever told you, you can fly, too."

Carmen finished cleaning and left, and all Holly could do for the rest of the evening was gaze out the window, the one that faced the pool. The underwater lights morphed smaller then bigger below the water and the small waves. The steam from the heated water rose delicately into the night.

And then she remembered something. A *somewhere* that wasn't her home, that was barely engraved in her modern memory, but that she'd kept hidden away, like a time capsule buried in the back yard, forgotten by the adult who put it there.

She rushed to her laptop, flipped it wide open. The screen glowed against her face, almost warmly like a fire, as she typed a name into Google. Why hadn't she remembered this place before now? It held her fondest memory from childhood. For her, it wasn't Christmas mornings, or luxurious vacations, or surprise birthday parties.

It was a place where she was sure a miracle happened.

Chapter Three

"You may call me Miss Bethany. And what may I call you?"

The older gentleman, bursting at the buttons with a life lived in excess, gave her a sideways glance, the kind only an outsider gives, she had noticed through the years. "The same name I told you five minutes ago. Lloyd."

"Well, you better listen, and you better listen closely."

Lloyd scoffed, pulling the toe of a shiny shoe against the concrete sidewalk and glancing at the hideous orange FOR RENT sign hanging in the dusty window.

Willow, who stood beside Miss Bethany, leaned in toward the man. "She's not kidding, you should listen."

"I did mention," this Lloyd said, "that I own real estate in Miami, New Orleans, and Santa Barbara."

"I see." Miss Bethany tapped her chin, gazing at him for a moment. "Well, we have ordinances here, Lance, and there is no budging."

"It's Lloyd, and let me assure you, these ordinances, whatever they are, can't possibly be as complicated as they are on Miami Beach."

"You'll notice the town is flawlessly decorated for Thanksgiving," Miss Bethany said. "Pumpkins galore. Scarecrows."

"Cornucopia," Willow added. "Nothing second-rate."

"Indeed." Miss Bethany said. She stepped closer to the man. "The entrance to the small town allows for a full view of its main shopping, dining, and rustic resort areas. At the top of the hill rests Victory Square, and the white gazebo over there is part of a small park, the setting of many weddings and the town's only place of worship, Victory Square Church."

The man snorted. "Well, I'm not much of a church go—" His gazed snapped to his feet as he caught her scowl. "I have noticed the, um, quaintness of your town, and how, um, religiously you've maintained your historical, Victorian look."

"Every shop complies," Miss Bethany said, peering at him over her reading glasses.

"This town must rake it in during Christmas!" he said.

"Not a light! Not a bow! Not a tree comes out

until precisely the day after Thanksgiving."

The man stepped back. He glanced at Willow, then back at Miss Bethany. "Are you kidding me? Revenues come in for Christmas starting in October. Why would you wait for Thanksgiving to arrive?"

"It is the way it is done. It is the way it was done. It is the way it will *always* be done." Miss Bethany glided her hand toward the empty shop. "So, what will it be? Are you interested or not?"

He turned and gazed at the shop, his hands stuffed in his pockets, slouching like his backbone suddenly fainted.

"Willow, hand him the ordinance book."

Willow took it out of her satchel and gave it to him.

He held it with two hands. "This must be three inches thick!"

"Perhaps Miami suits you better?"

"You're nuts. What a waste of time. Good luck with your itty-bitty town." He shoved the book back at Willow. "You'll be bankrupt without modern real estate ventures, ma'am. You can't stay in the past forever."

"We've been here for a hundred years, and we'll be here for a hundred more. Now, excuse yourself away — politely, I would ask — and get your car out of the no parking zone."

"No parking zone? It's the space in front of the shop."

"No cars blocking the shops, sir. We have a system, and you're not complying."

The man gave an unfriendly wave of his hand and left. Miss Bethany stayed put until his car was out of sight, then turned to Willow. "We must, Willow, fill this vacancy. It is such a gaping eye sore without anything in it, and that orange sign makes me want to boycott the color altogether. And please tend to the windows. So dusty, with children's fingerprints down here."

The delivery man, Roger, came out of the Welcome Center with a package and spotted them. "There you are, Miss Bethany. This came for you."

"Thank you."

"I like the outfit today," he said. "New?"

"Early bustle, circa 1872."

"It's working for you."

"Bye, Roger," Willow said, raising her hand far above her head, waving like the lunatics in Tennessee. Miss Bethany hated how the Tennessee folks waved, high above their heads, like a windshield wiper frantically trying to keep up with a heavy downpour of rain. But she tried to keep her opinions about that to herself. She had a lot of opinions about things, but the only ones that mattered now had to do with this beloved town.

"Willow," Miss Bethany said, "adjust your corset. We've got business. Very pressing business."

"Yes, ma'am. Yes, we do. What, um, is it that is

pressing?"

"How long have you been my assistant?"

"Eight weeks."

"Yes, eight weeks, that's right. You have a very easy name to remember. I know of no one else here named after a tree, except Larry's dog Bark."

"Oh, his name is actually Scoot—"

"It's Bark to me. The dog never sleeps or shuts up. But to my point, our business is that we must, *must*, fill this shop before Thanksgiving weekend."

She turned and headed west on Main, tearing the paper off the package and pushing the pieces into Willow's arms. She passed Ernie's Toy Store, suppressing a smile because smiles put people at ease and *at ease* never kept a town running. But Ernie did everything right. She particularly liked the stuffed pilgrims this year.

Next door was Oscar's General Store, and oh, what a scowl it brought to her face. This kind of senseless disregard for holiday could make even the sturdiest bustier fail. She peered through the front window, dark and desolate, not a fall decoration in sight.

"Where is...?"

Oscar's face appeared and peered right back at her, through the glass, causing her to gasp and hold her chest.

Next to her Willow chuckled, nothing the stink-eye couldn't kill on the spot. "Not funny, Willow.

Not funny. It's people like Oscar Menlow who could be the demise of this town, the old fart."

Oscar stepped into his doorway, a self-satisfied smirk sitting on top of his always hard-bitten expression.

"Oscar," Miss Bethany said, gripping the package close to her stomach, "you have exactly twenty-two minutes to put a scarecrow, Indian corn *with husks*, or dangling tissue-paper turkeys in that window, or I am fining you for insubordination." She began to turn, then turned back. "What happened to those cute little tissue-paper turkeys I gave you last year?"

Oscar stared at her, and she stared right back. The contest only lasted a moment before Oscar shrugged and Miss Bethany continued her inspection of the town, tearing off the rest of the shipping paper as she walked.

"I think he just likes getting a rise out of you, Miss Bethany," Willow said.

"Shush now. I've known Oscar for forty years, and he's as ornery as he ever was. And as grumpy too. What about that vacant shop, hmm? Any other bites?"

"I mean, yes, a couple. I thought this man today, Lloyd, would really be...well, anyway, clearly he was not right, but I've put a few more ads online. I used yummy adjectives like quaint and cozy. I even managed to work *whimsical* in there. And Victorian."

"You must learn not to babble."

"Yes, ma'am. I also mentioned the furnished apartment above it. Package deal, just like you asked."

"Our town isn't perfect unless *every* store is filled. It can't look like we're struggling economically." Miss Bethany paused, gazing toward the town square. Some tourists, a young family, were staring at the clock tower. "This season, Willow...it has to be perfect."

They walked on, Miss Bethany slowing for a moment to observe the Whistlestop Bed and Breakfast. "This..." She gave a sweeping gesture toward the building. "This is what we're all about. Look at this Victorian architecture and the three-sided veranda. And this yard! So lovely with the white picket fence. I particularly love the garland of fall leaves over the doorway this year."

"It fits right in," Willow said.

Miss Bethany watched the twins play catch in the yard. They were ten, with Lexie a nudge taller than Eli. Eli was the more imaginative one, wearing detective and cop costumes everywhere he went. Lexie was quite the sleuth herself, but tended to be more take-charge, the down-to-earth type.

"Hi, Miss Bethany!" Lexie said.

"Hi, Willow," Eli waved.

Willow started to return the wave, but Miss Bethany gently pushed her hand down. "Lexie, Eli, I have a job for you two."

The two hurried up to her, ready for their marching orders. Perhaps she wasn't the smiling sort, but these two made it hard not to grin.

"Go spy on Oscar. If he doesn't put up Thanksgiving decorations in the next twenty-one minutes, report to me."

"We'll snag digi proof," Lexie said.

"I don't know what that means, but I trust you."

"He won't get away with anything," Eli said with a salute. "Cop's honor!" He pulled out his spy glass from his pocket.

"Good. Now, skedaddle."

Miss Bethany pulled the rest of the paper off the box and then opened it up. "Ah! The new FOR RENT sign." She took it out and put the box into Willow's hands. "You see, dear, how much nicer this designer sign looks than that ugly orange one?"

"Oh yes, ma'am. Yes, indeed."

"Never, and I mean never, use one of those ugly signs again. The place that makes our signs is in the Rolodex."

"I just thought that sign would be a good one, since the other one went missing. Oscar gave it to me until we got a new one."

"I'll bet he did. After he stole the original. Has Sheriff Jackson slapped a fine on him yet?"

"Oscar said he didn't take it."

"Well, back we go to the store. We're putting it

up right away." Miss Bethany turned on her heel and headed east.

"I think it's on this side of cute, how much you and Oscar drive each other bonkers."

"Not another word. And we must work on your wave, dear. The way you wave, it's just so...well, a lesson for another time."

Willow hastily followed her, always a step behind. "So this store is such a catch, with the studio apartment above it! What do you see coming to life in that empty store?"

"I hope...I hope it's something that can bring this town together." Miss Bethany stopped in front of the window, staring at the glass that cast only her reflection in return.

Willow stepped beside her. "What do you mean?"

Miss Bethany studied her own image. Who was that staring back at her? She looked old, so serious, so...far away.

"Miss Bethany? Are you okay?"

Miss Bethany stepped away from the window, put the sign into the free fingers of her nervous assistant, and said, "The missing piece."

Willow nodded, and she knew the girl thought she spoke of the sign.

But she didn't.

Chapter Four

Holly couldn't remember the last time she'd been inside her little house on a weekday during the middle of the day. In pajama pants, no less! Was this it? Was this the nervous breakdown that she'd heard rumors of on Twitter, where the young, corporate elite suddenly throw everything away and buy a boat to live on?

It didn't feel like a nervous breakdown. She didn't feel at all sorrowful or depressed, even though she certainly had reason to. No, she felt…hopeful.

On her lap sat the keepsake box that once sat on her fireplace mantle, then on the coffee table, then in her dresser drawer. At some point it had ended up in a closet on the top shelf next to shoebox full of old cards.

Inside were photographs, weathered. Was she old enough to have weathered photographs? It seemed like just yesterday she was eight years old, yet she hardly recognized the young girl with the big grin, nestled in the arms of an attractive forty year old mother.

She held the photo up in the light. Behind them in the photo, a sign read *Whistlestop Bed & Breakfast*.

She picked up her laptop and put it in her lap, gazing at the picture on the screen. It was like not a day had gone by. There it was, a place that warmed her heart more than a single thing around here — or person, for that matter.

Her cell phone buzzed beside her. She didn't even glance at it. No, the world would not fall apart without her, though she was sure no one remembered her missing a day at work. She couldn't even remember the last time she'd missed.

Her attention back on her computer screen, she clicked the *reservations* tab. The Christmas she'd spent at this place was the best of her life. It was the only Christmas she could remember where it seemed like the world was as it should be.

A calendar popped up on her screen. She fell back against the cushions. Every day was X'd out. No vacancies.

She closed her eyes, trying to imagine what life would be like if she had Christmas there instead of here. She remembered the shops, each decorated perfectly, the Christmas lighting, the sweet little bed and breakfast. You could *hear* the Christmas music, and it wasn't just piped through stereo systems. People stood outside and *sang* the songs.

She decided to explore a little more and clicked on the town's website. What a beautiful, iconic place Bethany, Georgia, was! It was like a painting, one of those places you hope exists, but you never really know for sure.

Here it was, though, all twenty-first century with its snazzy website, but certainly the same as she remembered it.

Something caught her eye, an ad on the sidebar of the website.

Vacancy: One shop in need of a caring owner, apartment included. Quaint and cozy. Whimsical. Victorian. CLICK HERE for more information.

Then, as sudden as a burst of wind, her front door blew open without so much as a knock. Holly slammed her laptop shut, as if she'd been caught viewing something she shouldn't. Whoever stood in her doorway was backlit, hands on hips, and standing at about four foot eight. Breathing hard, too.

"Holliston?" came the smallish, squeaky-ish voice.

"Kinsey?"

The young girl moved into the room, hands still on her hips.

"Kinsey, what are you doing here?"

"What are *you* doing here?" She plopped down on the couch, eyeing the laptop. "It's the middle of the day. Are you sick? Because you don't look sick."

"No, not sick. Just playing hooky, as apparently you are as well." She raised a motherly eyebrow at Kinsey, though she was certain she wasn't pulling it off any more than Kinsey, who lifted a motherly eyebrow back at her.

"You never play hooky," Kinsey said. "And by the way you're gripping your laptop like it might just open itself up and bite you. I'm wondering what's going on here."

Holly loosened her grip. "They just let you out of seventh grade whenever you want?"

"I've got connections. Uncle Noah makes big donations to the school. He calls sometimes to let me out of the last hour because it's P.E. and I hate P.E. He has the principal's private cell phone and they text or something. I don't know. Anyway, I have to talk to you. I tried to ask Uncle Noah for some but he didn't have any. Literally, none. I have no choice but to come to you. But pa-*leaaaase* don't tell him I asked. It's a surprise."

"Kinsey, just so you're following, I have no idea what you're talking about."

"Well, good, because you're not supposed to. So far we've done our job. 'Til now. Oh boy. I'm ruining it!"

Alarm burst through Holly's body, partly because at twelve, Kinsey could have a drama queen meltdown nearly anywhere, and partly because she could sense that whatever Kinsey was about to tell her was going to ruin her day.

"Uncle Noah..." Kinsey began carefully, biting her fist for a moment like she was birthing words too painful to get out, "...no help there! None what-so-ever. Can you act surprised anyway?"

"If you clue me in. At this point, I'll be genuinely surprised, because I don't know—"

"I was given the task to edit the photo montage!" Kinsey blinked at her. "But my stupid uncle, well, he had *nothing*. Not even a single photo of you two alone."

Holly set her laptop down. "Why do you need photos of us?"

"I told you, to build the montage for...that part you're not supposed to know about."

"Oh...no..."

"I can't believe you'll be my aunt soon!" Kinsey's mood swung right up to glee, and Holly tried to adjust her expression, which she imagined held a good deal of dread.

"Oh, yes...uh..."

"Finally! 'Bout time my bone-headed, extraordinarily slow uncle proposed. He's marrying up, just so you know."

Holly attempted a smile but didn't think she succeeded. "Well, I guess you could say he proposed. He tried to make a transaction. I didn't say yes, Kinsey."

Kinsey's expression dropped.

"Yet." Holly tried to say it genuinely, as if there was hope, for Kinsey's sake.

"Well, you better, or this could get gossip-spready embarrassing. Like 'skirt tucked into your tights at the back while you walk around school' embarrassing. Not that I've done that. So sometime before tomorrow night—"

"Tomorrow night?" Holly leapt to her feet.

"Yeah. At the party. Keep up. Your engagement celebration."

"Who's throwing this party?"

"Your mother, of course. And Noah's parents. How can Uncle Noah not have any pics?" Kinsey stood and walked around the living area, presumably looking for some.

Holly grabbed her chest, then her belly, then her arms, sort of giving herself the feeling of a straitjacket.

She took two deep breaths, tried to keep up. "To be honest, Kinsey, I don't have any photos, either."

Kinsey slumped. "Hello? You guys have known each other since jelly bracelets were in style. How could you not have photos?"

"Just never had much of a reason to take them."

Suddenly Kinsey's whole demeanor changed, from bouncy pre-teen to dead-serious adult. "Holliston...we've got a problem, don't we?"

Holly's Adam's apple swelled double its size, right in her throat.

Chapter Five

Miss Bethany sat near the window, eating her lentil soup, but always watchful of what went on in her beloved town.

At Mom & Pop's, the town of Bethany's only diner, Lexie and Eli were ordering cream pies. Annalise Goodwin, possibly the town's only saint, asked the twins what had happened to the two she'd given them earlier, and they confessed they'd eaten them, and now their father had sent them back to get two more for his guests at the bed and breakfast.

"Babe?" she called to her husband, Christopher, who did all the cooking. "Do we have any more cream pies? Seems we've had some casualties."

"One banana, one chocolate," he called back.

Miss Bethany enjoyed watching the townspeople run their shops and loved seeing the tourists' faces. And the Goodwins always complied with all the codes. They made the extra effort to decorate their diner for every occasion. Though it probably qualified as a greasy spoon-type, with vinyl seats and a window where the food passed through to the waitresses, it had a certain quaintness to it—clean, shiny floors and pictures from the town's past hanging on every wall.

The bell dinged on the front door, and Willow floated in, whipping her head back and forth until she spotted her. Then she rushed over like there was something of urgent need. Miss Bethany set her spoon down. "What is it?"

"I think we have a renter for the shop and the apartment!"

Miss Bethany gestured to the chair opposite her as Willow handed her the papers. "Willow, do sit and lower your voice. We must absorb ourselves into the town, not stick out like sore thumbs."

Willow glanced down at her Victorian dress.

"Besides the outfits, Willow. Now, what is the matter?"

"Nothing, nothing at all! Just look. She seems perfect."

Miss Bethany put on her reading glasses and reviewed the papers. "Well, her credit checks fine."

"And she's very nice. She seemed so eager."

"I suppose we'll go ahead and approve her. What choice do we have? It's seven days until Thanksgiving. You did tell her she must be ready by Thanksgiving?"

"I did. She promised she'd have store ideas to

ask you about as soon as she arrives."

"All right. Give her the go ahead."

Willow bit her lip. "Already done, ma'am. She's on her way."

Miss Bethany gave Willow a stern look, but perhaps it was the right move. They were desperate to fill the vacancy. Willow, despite her jittery nature, was proving herself to be a good assistant.

"Very well, then. Let's make the announcement."

Willow went to the counter, got the bell from Annalise, and rang it as Miss Bethany took center stage, eyeing Liam's children, who were now sitting at a table, a bit filthy, eating chicken fried steak with their fingers. Eli was drinking his soda with a spoon.

"Listen up, folks. We have a newbie coming. We need to give her that Bethany welcome, help her set up for the big event. Everything's gotta be perfect this year."

"Isn't it always, Miss Bethany?" Christopher said from behind her. She turned. Annalise stood by his side.

"Yes, for you two. Yes. But I mean for the whole town. For us all. Please wrap me a piece of apple pie to go."

Nearby, Oscar was watching her, his arms folded.

* * *

Holly had thirteen messages on her phone, which dinged every once in awhile to remind her that she'd left a whole world behind. She had moments of panic as her trip stretched into hours. She'd never done anything like this before. As a teen, she was the one who came home right on time, sometimes early just to make sure. But Carmen's words rang in her ear. *Her* wishes mattered. *Her* life plan mattered. She didn't want Noah. She didn't want her dad's corporation. She didn't want to be stuck in that life forever.

As she'd peeled out of the driveway of her home, ignoring the guests arriving for the engagement party, she'd spotted Carmen in the window, smiling at her. She kept that picture in her head as she drove.

She'd decided to turn back about twenty times. Fleeing was not her nature. But somehow she kept going, stopping at scenic views along the way, snapping pictures, each one giving her more resolve than the last.

Maybe it was a bunch of things over the last two years that led to her realization that Noah was not for her, but perhaps the tipping point was the moment she realized she had no pictures of the two of them. And maybe this was why at each scenic point, she snapped a furious amount of pictures, maybe to fill in the gaps where she and Noah should have been.

Only one radio station came in on the Appalachian Highway as she continued to drive toward this new town she was to call home, and at one point, they played *Go Tell It on the Mountain*. That's what she hummed for the rest of the drive.

As she came over the hill, she saw it. It sat in the valley, nearly shining. She approached slowly, taking in all the details. The tall trees and green, green grass. One road led in, taking her straight to the center of the town, where every shop was decorated to a Thanksgiving theme, just like she remembered as a child, though when she was there, it was Christmas. The sidewalks were swept. There was not a tumbling piece of trash in sight.

She easily spotted the shop she'd leased. It was the only vacant one she could see. Above it was the window of the new apartment. The building was precious with its clapboard siding and upper gable windows. Several signs instructed her as to where she shouldn't park, but she found a space that said "loading zone, 15 minutes," so she figured that was the right place for her.

She called the woman she spoke to, Willow, letting her know she'd arrived. Holly then sat in her car waiting and listened to the voice messages that had come through along her way here. Her mother was angry. Her father was worried. Noah had not bothered to even call...he just texted: *?????*

She glanced up to see a horde of people filing

out of what looked like the Welcome Center, an older woman cautiously trailing behind them. It had to be Miss Bethany, whom Willow described as having a "non-negotiable" personality.

She donned a Victorian dress but without the slow, soft stroll of the women in that era who wore them.

Holly stepped out of her SUV and smoothed out her skirt and shirt. To her left she noted the Toy Store, where an older, kind-looking, roly-poly man peered out the window at her. Next to the Toy Store was a General Store, not as lavishly decorated as the rest, but in the window hung a solitary, colorful tissue-paper turkey.

Outpacing the tiny crowd tumbling toward her was a very kind, pretty woman, extending her hand long before she even reached Holly. She looked to be in her forties.

"You must be Holly!" the woman said, finally reaching her, shaking her hand vigorously. "I'm Annalise." She pointed behind Holly. "My husband Chris and I run that diner over there. And we insist, first meal is on the house."

"Oh, wonderful. Thank you."

Out of the corner of her eye, Holly saw something move, but when she looked toward the tree and nearby mailbox, there was nobody there. She returned her attention to the crowd in front of her.

"I love all the Thanksgiving décor," Holly said.

"I'm Willow," the young woman beside Annalise said. She also wore a Victorian outfit, but with chunky, modern glasses and a modern bob. "We spoke on the phone. But don't get too attached to this décor. Per Miss Bethany's explicit instructions." She waved her hand around, and gestured toward the older lady. "It's all leaving at the stroke of midnight on Thursday. That's when we morph into Christmas Town."

By the way she said *stroke of midnight* she knew these people were serious.

Miss Bethany had disappeared. Holly looked around and spotted her. She was peering inside Holly's SUV.

"You don't have near enough to fill this store."

"I have a shipment on the way."

Miss Bethany glanced at the delicate, antique wristwatch on her arm, which complimented her Victorian dress well. "And you've got twelve more minutes before you have to park elsewhere."

"Have you owned a store before, Holly?" Annalise asked.

"Nope. I was manager of my dad's company, but this is way different." She paused, unable to keep the smile from cracking through. "Thank heavens."

"So, what will this place be?" Annalise asked.

All three of them looked at her expectantly, and

then she figured out what she'd seen moving nearby: two children, dressed as...spies? At least one of them was, but the other held a spyglass up to her eye. It seemed they were willing to blow their cover to hear what she had to say.

"Well," Holly said, feeling a bit like she was in a boardroom pitching her new idea without a PowerPoint presentation. "I spent time online, looking at what you guys already have. I really want to bring something here that this place needs. There was this store you guys had twenty years ago...it was called Lily's Memories. It was closed when I..."

Her voice trailed off as she noticed Miss Bethany reached out to grab something. There was nothing beside her but air. Had she said something wrong?

The woman recovered quickly, though her face had lost some of its color. "You've been here before?"

Holly turned toward the empty window. "I have. I remember as a child staring through the window, wishing it were still open."

"So you're opening a scrapbooking store?" Annalise asked.

"That's right. Holly's Hobbies. To start off with, I want a place for people to capture memories worth keeping. Have hobby nights with tourists and locals, where we all get together and scrapbook." She turned toward them. "Create a sense of community, just like your town. Eventually I want to branch off to include all sorts of hobbies and crafts."

There was sure a mixed bag of expressions between the ladies standing there. She couldn't tell if they liked it or not. She had the idea of bringing in a machine that quickly printed digital pictures from phones, iPads, and digital cameras, right there on the spot, but maybe they weren't ready to hear that. She clasped her hands together and turned toward Miss Bethany. "Willow mentioned you need to approve whatever type of store I'd like to run. Would that, I mean...does that fit in, Miss Bethany?"

Willow and Annalise turned to look at the old woman too, whose face had now dropped into total neutrality. But instead of answering, she only turned and walked back to the Welcome Center, her Victorian dress appearing to drag the ground, as if she'd just lost a little bit of her height.

"It'll be just fine, Holly," Willow said, gently touching her hand. The woman met her eyes, then hurried after Miss Bethany.

Holly turned to Annalise. "What did I say?"

"Lily was Miss Bethany's daughter." The *was* hung heavy in the air.

"Oh dear. I'm sorry. I had no idea. Do I need to rethink this whole thing?"

Annalise didn't seem concerned. "You have just the right idea, Holly. You may be just what the town of Bethany needs. I have to go, but you holler at me if you need anything, okay?"

Suddenly, as if on cue, there was a bit of hollering. A man had stepped out the front door of the bed and breakfast and was motioning to the spy kids. He crouched down just in time for them to run into his arms. He lifted them both and took them inside.

"That's Liam," Annalise said. "He owns the bed and breakfast. Those are his two kids, Lexie and Eli. Keep an eye on them…if you can. They like to spy."

"I, uh, noticed that."

Soon Holly was left on the sidewalk all by herself. She took a deep breath and turned back to the storefront. Through the window, all she saw was an opportunity for a new life. It was going to be a lot of hard work, but she knew it would be worth it and she felt—

"One minute, thirty seconds of parking left!" The voice pierced the air. There was no one in sight, but she already knew who it belonged to. Miss Bethany.

Chapter Six

She'd spent three nights working already and still had some things to unpack. Though she barely fit inside the bathroom of her new apartment, she loved the place. She'd had big and expansive, and it was not all it was cracked up to be. When she was a child, before she'd moved into the guest apartment on her parents' property, her bathroom was the size of this entire place. Friends would come over and fawn over the space, but she always felt tiny and insecure there, like the whole thing might swallow her up one day.

She slathered her face with exfoliating cream, pushing strands of hair out of her eyes that had fallen from the messy bun on top of her head.

She was appreciating the hush of night in this town when she heard a *thump* and then a *bump*. It wasn't the friendly kind, if such a thing existed. It sounded as ominous as a noise in the night could sound.

Tripping over boxes, suitcases, and bags she'd yet to unpack, she stumbled toward the door as she wiped the cream off her hands on a dishtowel sitting on the coffee table. She opened the door, then realized she had nothing to defend herself with — other than the hideous look of a woman attempting to fight age at twenty-eight. She brushed more hair out of her face and grabbed the wooden spoon sticking out of the box next to the door.

The indoor staircase behind the shop that led up to her apartment had seemed so quaint earlier in the day, when the sun was out and the birds were chirping. It was small, made from old wood, and had all the character you'd expect from this town. Now, though, in the dark, with a single light bulb illuminating the steps, it might as well be steps to a dungeon.

The spoon was held high above her head, clearly announcing that she really had no defense whatsoever. Once she reached ground floor, she could see the lights were on in the store. The sounds of shuffling and knocking and bumping filtered through the closed door. Pushing the door slightly open, she saw them — four men moving around with purpose.

Well, she thought, *nothing like the element of SURPRISE!*

She pushed the door all the way open, and it banged against the wall.

The noise didn't have quite the effect she was hoping for. The four men turned, stared at her. Nobody jumped or looked the least big guilty. She quickly lowered the spoon to her side.

"Who are you people?" she asked, though she recognized two of them — one from the Toy Store, one from the bed and breakfast.

"Hello, purdy lady," the Toy Store man said, a kindly grin stretched across his rotund face. "What'cha got there?" He pointed to her spoon.

"I was in the middle of cooking?" Gosh, that was not supposed to come out as a question.

"Covered in face soap?" the handsome bed and breakfast man asked.

"I'm into clean cooking."

"Eating," he said.

"Yes, that. Clean eating."

Her face was starting to burn. The cream was to be left on precisely five minutes, but she was drawn to the man smiling at her, seemingly amused, who ran the bed and breakfast.

"Battle Axe sent us," one of the men said. She hadn't met this one.

"Who?" she asked.

The Toy Store man said, "What Oscar meant to say was the lovely and delightful Miss Bethany sent us."

"Don't be puttin' wrong words in my mouth," Oscar said with a growl.

Handsome man stepped forward, held out a hand. "I'm Liam Price. I run the Whistlestop Bed and Breakfast next door. Miss Bethany asked us to make shelves for your big shipment. And when I say asked, I mean told. Not that we mind."

Holly gripped her spoon with both hands. She'd wondered how she was going to get shelves up. "Wonderful! Thank you! She didn't tell me."

"I'm Ernie," said the Toy Store owner. "That's the way it is 'round here. We just all pitch in. Say, if you ever want to play a game of Yahtzee, come on over to my store."

"And I'm Christopher," said the other man. "I'm Annalise's husband. And you'll just have to get used to the fact that I smell like chicken fried steak all the time."

"Ooo! I love chicken fried steak." She glanced at Liam. "When, of course, I'm not clean eating."

"What in the world is clean eating?" Oscar asked. "One of those crazy fads where you only eat soap?"

Holly liked these fellows already. "Does this town have a police department? You know, in case one of these nights it's not my friendly neighbors nosing around. Unannounced."

"If a one-man show makes a department," Ernie shrugged. "His name's Sheriff Jackson."

"You can catch him cat-napping between nine and five at the station right by our diner,"

Christopher said, handing Liam a drill. "He's got a pager for middle of the night calls."

Holly smiled at the word *pager*.

"But no worries," Liam said. "You won't need it here in Bethany. And I'm right next door to you if you need anything." He put the drill bit in the drill. "So what brings you here?"

She noticed his eyes, a deep hazel with green specs. Was she staring? She really should rush upstairs and wash the cream off. Her skin was stinging like an awful sunburn. But for some reason, she just didn't want to.

"Let's just say," she answered, "I wanted to come to a place where I could be my own boss, make my own decisions for once."

"Well," Oscar said with a huff, "you certainly picked the wrong place. You seen the size of Bethany's ordinance manual? Gives *Gone with the Wind* a run for its page count."

Yes, the ordinance book had indeed been delivered to her by Willow, about an hour after she'd arrived.

Now her face burned like the sun was cozying up to her. "Well, men, thank you again for this. If there is anything you need, I'll be right upstairs."

They all smiled and nodded, but Liam held her gaze for a moment longer than everyone else. She blushed, but nobody could see it through the cream and what was surely becoming a ruddy complexion.

She sauntered out, but as soon as she closed the door, she bolted upstairs like a wildcat and again, stumbling over boxes and bags, made her way to the bathroom where she vigorously splashed her face. As soon as the cream was off, the air to her skin felt great...for a moment. Then she saw her complexion...what was left of it. Her whole face was the color of a Red Delicious apple.

"Yikes..." She leaned into the mirror.

Out in her apartment, she dug through one of her bags and found her aloe vera. She slathered it a half inch thick, then sighed as the gel cooled her face.

Exhausted, she knew she didn't have enough strength to unpack the rest of her things, so she changed into her pajamas and crawled into the daybed that the apartment had come furnished with. It was time, she knew, to listen to the messages that had poured in from her family. At some point she was going to have to call them, tell them she was all right, explain herself a little.

Tonight was not the night.

But she did listen to a few of the messages, including one from her mother. Her mother's voice sounded like the strained pitch of a cat meowing for food. "Holliston, whatever you're trying to do, you know it's just not going to work. Come home. We'll make things right for you."

She shut her phone down and held it to her chin. "No, Mother, right for *you*."

She slept restlessly. The new bed and her eagerness to get on with this new life kept her mind from ever fully relaxing.

As morning came, the sun streamed in through the window, and she was certain the light here glowed differently, more warmly. She made a simple breakfast...a fried egg and plain toast...thanks to some wonderful staples that were stocked in her fridge before she'd arrived, accompanied by a note that read, "Welcome to Bethany!" She then got busy downstairs. She was delighted to see all the shelves waiting for her. Those shelves she took as a sign that she had Miss Bethany's blessing to go forward with a scrapbooking shop, however painful it was for the woman to see.

By noon Holly's back was hurting and knotted, and her face still burned, though most of the redness had gone. She now just looked like she was perpetually blushing, and even the best makeup couldn't cover it. But she had more serious things on her mind. She knew this town was counting on her to get her store in order.

Holly had decided late last night that this store would be a blessing to this town and, more importantly, to Miss Bethany.

By three, she had her tables set up, and her scrapbooking supplies were delivered right on time that afternoon. Her vision was coming together, and she could even imagine the people in here, delighting in their memories, enjoying each other's memories.

That image brought to mind another one—herself and her own photographs, or lack thereof. It wasn't just photos she was missing, though. It was memories. She didn't have enough of her own to fill a book...none that she'd want to save, anyway. None that changed her life in a good way. All of her recent memories, all of the snapshots of her life, brought to mind nothing but disappointment.

"To new memories," she said to herself.

The front door opened. Annalise came in, trailed by an older woman.

"Hi Holly! I have a break. I thought I'd help you clean and get ready."

"That is so nice, Annalise."

"And this is Gladys Eisley. She works with Liam, cooking and baking for the bed and breakfast when needed."

Gladys set a tray of goodies down. "Holly, we are so glad you're here. So glad. My husband owns the Toy Store."

"Ernie! Yes! He built some sturdy shelves for me." Holly patted the one next to her.

"He has his moments," she said with a wink. "God bless him. When he's willing to stop playing Yahtzee long enough."

The front door opened again, the little bell

announcing Miss Bethany, who clearly had no plans for niceties. Her demeanor was all business. She held two packages in her hand.

"I ordered you a sign that complies with the Bethany Town Code. I will tack it on your rent bill. Don't forget to fill out your business license app and pay the fees."

Miss Bethany put the package on the table, glancing nonchalantly around the room, unwilling to let any approving expression through. Then she began to rip the paper off the package, handing it to the air behind her, where nobody stood to grab it before it flittered to the floor. Before long, the sign became visible. She held it up for Holly to see.

Holly's Hobbies

Holly put a hand to her mouth, and tears rushed to her eyes. "It's perfect, Miss Bethany. Just perfect. It's a dream come true."

Miss Bethany regarded her for a moment. Some unspoken thought seemed to play across her face, but she was unwilling to say it. Instead she handed Holly the sign, then pointed to the other box. "This other one here, you'll put in the window at the stroke of midnight, after Thanksgiving."

"Yes, ma'am."

Miss Bethany left, and Annalise and Gladys clapped their hands.

"Hang it, dear!" Gladys said.

Annalise nodded, her eyes bright with

anticipation.

"Okay, here it goes."

The window was already constructed to hold a sign just the size of the one she held in her hand, so with ease, she hung it. "Dreams coming true, right there!" Gladys said with a triumphant gesture.

"And a life left behind, too," Holly said quietly.

Chapter Seven

Jf there were another town so quaint, traditional and lovely, Holly wouldn't believe it to exist. Earlier in the evening, she'd witnessed a town coming together to enjoy the Thanksgiving feast. The *whole* town. The diner was converted into a banquet hall, and everyone pitched in. Someone brought green bean casserole. Some brought pies. And everyone helped pull tables together. The end result was a warm, inviting, celebratory occasion that brought the best, it seemed, out of everyone. She even witnessed it when, with great chivalry, Oscar pulled a chair out for Miss Bethany. And she thought she witnessed Miss Bethany almost smile, though she wouldn't testify to that in court.

Holly didn't bring anything to eat. She was still unpacking her apartment, due to how hard she'd been working on the store. But she did bring a Thanksgiving Day Guest Book in which everyone could sign their names and favorite memory of the day.

Annalise thought it was a terrific idea.

A hand grabbed hers. She looked down to find one of the twins, the girl, tugging at her arm. "Please join us! My dad said to ask nicely, but I'm pretty bossy, and I really want you to sit with us, so…"

Holly laughed. "Well, I don't have any family here, so I appreciate that. Thank you."

"My name is Lexie, in case you forgot. Brother is Eli. Dad is Liam. That's it, so…" She tugged at her arm. "Come on, what'cha waiting for?"

"Let me grab some tea. I'll be right there."

Lexie bounded off, and Holly looked toward Liam, who cracked a smile and waved her over. She nodded and went to the table covered with plastic cups filled with tea. What a completely different experience this was from the Thanksgivings she was used to. Back home, Thanksgiving seemed to be more of a networking opportunity than anything else. Even as a child, she was strictly instructed to behave and be quiet at the table. She was always dressed for the occasion, and a week beforehand, Carmen was instructed to go over all the etiquette with her. Only the adults were allowed to talk. As she grew into a teen, her mother reminded her that it was not a day to *pig out*. "Portion control," she instructed, "should always be front and center in your mind."

She walked to the end of the table where Liam

and his family sat. Eli pulled out a chair for her, seating her right next to Liam.

"Thank you for the invitation," she said.

"Of course. How is the store going?"

"I'm ready to open tomorrow."

He laughed. "It must seem so silly to you."

"Not at all. I love this. I love all of it. That's why I'm here. I needed to leave a...very complicated life."

"I see," he said, but a bewildered tilt of his head said otherwise.

Miss Bethany rang a bell that quieted everyone down. Ernie was asked to say the blessing, and it seemed that was a very honored tradition, as even the children settled down and hushed. They all joined hands. Ernie's prayer was less wordy and more emotion. His gratitude was apparent, and when he asked God to bless their little town and keep it going, Holly felt a somberness in her soul, a need to join her voice with the others who were agreeing and saying, "Amen."

She used to go to church, as a child, until a business deal went bad with her father and one of the deacons. They never went again.

As soon as Ernie finished, the room erupted in conversation, laughter, and the clanging of dishes. Hordes of food were passed from person to person.

Eli eyed her plate. "You sure don't eat very much."

Holly smiled. "You think I should eat a bit

more?"

"A bit?" Lexie asked. "At the end of the evening, my dad says you should be so stuffed you gotta unbutton your pants."

Liam laughed sheepishly. "Well, um, something like that. It's a festive time."

"I agree." Holly plopped an extra spoonful of potatoes on her plate. "How's that?"

Lexie shrugged. "It should mound, but you're a newbie, so we'll teach you later. You can't skip the pie, though."

"Oh, you got it. I never skip pie."

Lexie smiled and looked at her dad. "I told you she was likable."

Liam shook his head and stared at his plate. "Sorry. She's a little, um, forthcoming."

Holly winked at the little girl. "Don't ever change, okay?" She liked her, so opposite of herself. She'd been taught never to speak her mind.

The kids engaged in conversation with others and Liam looked at her. "Do you miss being with your family on Thanksgiving?"

"Not at all," she smiled. "This is exactly what I'm looking for."

"Well, we are, indeed, a family. A very big...and loud...one," he said, just as the crowd at a nearby table roared with laughter. "Your store looks to be coming along. I think it's going to be a hit. What a perfect time to launch, too, during the

holidays. You'll be amazed by the number of visitors
that come through here during Christmas time."

"So who is the biggest Christmas nut around
here?" Holly asked.

His chuckle was deep and inviting. "Besides
Miss Bethany?"

"Yes. Clearly she should be crowned."

"Well, that's a hard one. Everyone has a special
thing they love about it, and it's reflected in how
they decorate and what they do with their
businesses." He took a bite of turkey, then a sip of
his tea. "Are you a fan of Christmas?"

"I am now." A grin escaped she could hardly
contain.

"Hmm. Mysterious one, you are."

She shrugged. "Not really. It's just that my
family...well, let's say the emphasis is always
around my father's business. He uses every holiday
to make a connection or throw a party for a client or
whatever. It's just very different than...this."

"So, while coming to Bethany, you're also
running away?"

"Maybe," she said. "But I'm fully committed to
being here, to making this work."

"I can tell," he said.

"How?" she asked.

"Because Miss Bethany hasn't run you off. She's
how we vet everyone."

"Well, I can say that meeting her was more

intense than any job interview I've been on." She tried a smile, because the truth was, she'd never had a job interview. She'd worked for her father nearly her whole life. She had memories of bringing him paper from the copier at age five.

This new experience was completely different. A lot was expected from her, sure, but she was giving a lot too. And she'd always wondered if she could make it on her own.

She and Liam chatted during dinner. She didn't ask about a wife. He wasn't wearing a ring. He had very intense, life-filled eyes, and she tried not to get swept away by them. She'd just left one man. She needed to give her heart a rest for awhile.

Pie was served later, and everyone was in high spirits when finally Miss Bethany got the people's attention and beckoned the entire room outside. Holly trailed the crowd. The town gathered around the clock tower that stood in the middle of the town square.

Christmas music was piped through an ancient sound system. The night, festive down below, was quiet and sparkling overhead. At twenty-five minutes until midnight, all the shop owners were given their marching orders. Everyone was prepared.

And as the clock struck midnight, a roar of clapping and shouting was accompanied by beautiful lights glowing through the darkness, large nativity scenes decorating sidewalks and shop corners, reindeers hanging in windows and new signs appearing everywhere. The diner now read *Mr. and Mrs. Claus Diner*. The toy store was now to be called *The Elves Toy Shop*. The General Store hung a sign that read, *Oh Come All Ye Spenders*. It wasn't quite like the others, but it seemed the best Oscar could do.

Next door, Liam hung his sign, changing out *Whistlestop Bed & Breakfast* to *Mistletoe B&B*. The twins hung garland and mistletoe above the door.

Holly watched it all from her store front. And right on cue, she hung her own sign in the window: *Deck the Hollies*.

* * *

At the Welcome Center, the shop owners trailed in, as was tradition, for hot apple cider and Christmas cookies, which Gladys always did a wonderful job of making. Miss Bethany stood by the door, nodding at each of them. The town looked lovely, she thought. All the lamp posts were wrapped in white lights, strung from top to bottom. The town's nativity scene was secured in the center, on the piece of lawn that was meticulously maintained all year round for this very occasion. Last year Mary's hand broke off, but it was fixed and looked as good as new now.

Holly, the newcomer, smiled at her as she

passed by. Miss Bethany had strolled by Holly's store several times through the evening, and it surpassed her expectations. The boughs of holly, used as trim around the front bay window, was an especially nice touch. And when she pointed out to the young lady that there was a gum wad in the crack of the sidewalk, without hesitation, Holly got to scraping away.

It was a good start, but one season a shop owner did not make. It was yet to be seen whether Holly had what it took to own a shop in the town of Bethany.

Willow brought Miss Bethany the traditional first cup of cider in her beloved snowman mug, and Miss Bethany raised her glass to the crowd, who raised their paper reindeer cups in return.

"Folks, you've done it again!"

Cheers and hoorays.

"Now, how about we get us some of that shut eye?" Oscar said. "It's three a.m."

"I'm not finished, Oscar." She looked at Holly. "Holly, the rule is that you must show up for work tomorrow—"

"—and by tomorrow she means today—" Oscar grumbled.

"—in your Christmas pajamas. Seven-thirty sharp."

Willow said, "We've got a spare pair for if you haven't any."

"Sounds comfy!" Holly said.

Nearby she noticed Liam smiling at Holly.

"Folks," she continued, "people who come here expect an experience. It's why we get so many repeat tourists. Let's give them a Christmas season to remember. May this year..." And then a strange thing happened, a thing that she couldn't remember happening since...

She choked on emotion.

"Miss Bethany?" Willow said, tilting her head.

Miss Bethany waved her off. "May this year be our most memorable year ever."

"Here, here!" said the crowd.

Like Oscar's mood changes, Annalise was right by her side in a flash, holding up the traditional red bucket, reaching her hand in, swirling her fingers around. Nearby, she heard Willow explaining the red bucket to Holly.

"Each year, we draw names rather than getting a present for each person. Rule is we buy local."

Annalise leaned toward Miss Bethany, whispering in her ear. "Did we forget to make name cards?"

But even that whisper was heard by everyone, who stared at Miss Bethany, eyes wide, like she'd just announced Santa had died.

Miss Bethany tipped her chin up, the way she always did when she had an important announcement to make.

"This," she said in the voice that carried so well through a room, "is one tradition we're changing up this year. We are not going to pick names."

The murmuring started right away, except for Oscar, she noticed, who wasn't capable of murmuring if his life depended on it. "Well! Wonders never cease, woman! Didn't know you had it in you to deviate from tradition."

"No lip from any of you!" Miss Bethany said, and it was harsher than she'd intended. Though she tried to keep a steady expression, she knew there were some in the crowd who understood the breaking of this tradition meant something was wrong.

She swallowed her emotion, a big gulp of it like that summertime raspberry iced tea that she liked, but Oscar caught her eye, and they stared at each other for a moment, the kind of stare that felt like he was looking right into her soul. His eyes, normally every shade of harsh, were soft with concern.

She looked away, shooing them all with her hand. "Go, now. Go count a few sheep."

Still perplexed, they all wandered out, some leaving their cider and cookies behind.

Annalise slowly handed her the red bucket. "Oh, my, Miss Bethany. This was one of my favorite traditions."

"Just, um, keeping everyone on their toes. Maybe new traditions need to be made. We have a whole new generation of Bethany-ites coming up, true?"

Annalise only shrugged and said, "Have a good night."

Oscar was the last one out of the room, as he'd been holding the door for everyone to leave, though not happily. He took one last look at Miss Bethany.

"What is it? Have I grown a second nose?"

Oscar raised an eyebrow. "No. But maybe a longer one." And he slipped quietly out.

Chapter Eight

Decked out in her new reindeer pajamas, the softest material she'd ever had the pleasure of wearing, Holly tiptoed quietly across the property that was clearly marked "No Trespassing." It was nearly four a.m., and there was not a quieter time in the night. The stars had even dimmed, which made it hard to see. Every footstep seemed ten times louder than it really was. Or at least than she'd hoped it was. Otherwise, she'd be caught for sure.

Wrapping her coat tightly around her and holding the small shovel she'd purchased two days ago from Oscar, she managed to make it over the small picket fence that divided their properties. It was so small, she wasn't sure if it would keep a Yorkie in place, but it worked wonderfully for her purposes.

Her coat got caught between slats, and she had to wriggle free, and not in the quietest of ways. But she commanded herself to stay on task. Glancing around, she saw all the windows nearby, and in particular at the bed and breakfast, were still dark, so she tiptoed across the lawn again, a little proud of her prowler instincts, since she'd assumed she had none whatsoever.

Through the dark, the Christmas lights that were up and glowing at the B&B provided enough light for her to see the exact spot she needed, under the tree that seemed much smaller now than she remembered from childhood.

Taking a deep breath, she looked around one more time and then began to dig. It was much harder than she'd imagined. She couldn't remember ever using a shovel, and surely there was a technique to it. Whatever that technique was, she wasn't getting it, because she was pulling up about a quarter of an inch of dirt at a time.

"You know, seven-thirty will be here in no time, right?"

A gasp, a loss of balance, and a quick fall to the ground caused a delay in Holly turning to see who was behind her.

"Liam...uh, hi..."

"Hi there."

"This probably seems very strange."

"What's that?" He pointed to the shovel.

"Oh, this. Yes, um, this is a shovel. From Oscar's store. He gave me the newcomer special." She sighed. Yes, sure, *that's* information he wanted...she got it at a bargain.

Liam put his hands in his pockets. He was dressed in jeans...not pajama bottoms like herself.

"And you are digging up my formerly flawless yard because...?"

"It is a lovely yard." She stood and grasped her shovel again because she needed something to hold on to. "Shouldn't you be sleeping?"

"Shouldn't you?"

For an unknown reason, she was compelled to keep digging, right there in front of the man on whose property she was trespassing. But she might not get another chance. She tried to keep talking.

"Yeah, that. Me, adrenaline. So much adrenaline. Opening my store tomorrow, well, today...sleep is not happening."

"So coming here, digging up my yard, that was clearly the better option."

"Well, of course, because..."

She was digging so fast, she hardly noticed the great progress she made until suddenly her shovel hit metal.

"There it is!"

"Treasure?" Liam asked casually. "Because I'm going to need a cut of that. It's on my property. You're stealing."

She laughed. "Not treasure, at least to anyone else. And technically, I'm not stealing. This is mine. Your property was just holding it for me for twenty years."

"Ah."

Holly pulled the small metal box out of the earth as Liam watched.

"This," she said, "is all of a girl's hopes and dreams."

"And they fit in one dirty, metal box. You dream big."

Holly carefully unlatched it. It practically twinkled in the light of the Christmas lights. She pulled out small slips of paper and smiled. She held out the box to Liam. He stared at it a moment, then took it from her.

"Miss Bethany...helped me bury it right here," Holly said, shuffling through the papers, reading each one. "She convinced me the dreams would grow." She winked at him. "So if you want to blame someone for this mess, blame her."

"Well, she does own this soil. Did you stay here? In this B&B?"

"When I was eight years old, I came into town with my parents to celebrate Christmas."

Liam peered deeper into the box.. "So...what made the list?"

"My Ken," she laughed.

Even in the dim light, she could see his eyebrow lift.

"You know. I'd be Barbie to my Ken."

"Ah. Him. The one no eight-year-old boy can live up to."

"Yeah," Holly laughed. "Such a fantasy, we all find out when we grow up. Here's another one. *My own store.*"

She looked at Liam, who seemed genuinely touched. "You dreamed about that back then?"

"I even told my parents I wanted it to be here. They laughed at me. Of course, I can't blame them. It was going to be the Barbie and Ken store."

"You should know, I would not have shopped there."

"So much for loyalty." She read another. "Hmm. *A peaceful home life.*"

"You didn't already have that?"

"Well, I didn't write this expecting it from my parents. I meant my own."

"So...you're batting one out of three."

"Sometimes one dream can make up for all others, wouldn't you say?"

"I can only hope you're right about that." He paused, looking into the box. "Was that the only time you came to Bethany?"

"Yes. It was the one Christmas my parents planned something without the nanny. My grandmother had died. Mom, she wanted to get away. But they almost ruined it. After we got here, it became about the greasy food. The lumpy beds. The ironing method the maids must have used on the sheets." She grinned at him. "Have you changed your ironing methods, Mr. Whistlestop?"

"I had no idea I was supposed to iron the sheets."

Holly grimaced a little. Yeah...most people didn't iron their sheets.

"I tried so hard to just savor time with them alone," she continued, "and they made everyone miserable." Holly laughed at the memory. "Miss Bethany...she let 'em have it."

Liam raised an eyebrow. "Sounds like Miss Bethany."

"Yep. Oh my goodness. She tried to get them to see they needed to appreciate the family they had. And it actually worked. For a while."

"How did you end up coming back here?"

"That's actually your fault."

He ducked his head in mock-humility. "Please accept my sincerest apologies."

"I was looking for a place to escape for Christmas, but good ole Whistlestop had no vacancies. Then I saw Willow's ad for the store, and something clicked."

Suddenly in the darkness, a light popped on down the way. Between the buildings, she could see another. Liam smiled at her. "The day starts early here in Bethany during Christmas season. Everyone gets up and gets going."

"Well, then, I best prowl myself back to my apartment and get ready." She couldn't help the grin. "I'm so excited about this day! And nervous too. I sure hope someone comes into my store. Oh, and my sincerest apologies for the, um, gaping hole in the ground."

"Apology accepted. And don't worry. It gets crazy around here. People love Bethany. They come in droves. And if it means anything, I think your idea for your store is...perfect." He handed her the box back. "Also, use the gate. It's safer."

She blushed, imagining him watching her scale his little fence. "Right. Thank you. And I will fix the hole, I promise."

"Don't worry about it. I'll put the kids on it."

"Thank you. Good night. I mean, good morning." She suppressed a laugh at her own idiocy. What an impression she must be making. Holly trailed back to her property, clutching the box with all her dreams, but with her mind on the man standing by the hole she'd just dug.

Chapter Nine

The last time Holly remembered feeling this unnerved was when she'd taken her SATs. Outside the window of her shop, the town was springing to life—eager customers, ready to shop, grabbing breakfast first at the diner.

She stepped outside with her broom and swept the sidewalk in front, just like Oscar and Ernie were doing. Down the way, she saw Miss Bethany and Willow waving at tourists, their Victorian pantaloons peeking out the bottom of their dresses.

Once the sidewalk was clean, she walked inside and put on her antlers, then surveyed the room. Everything was in place. Albums and paper were on the south wall. Stickers, organized by themes, were in the display cases. And all the supplies anyone could need for scrapbooking were on the east walls. The tables sat in the middle, and luckily the store had come with a cash register—possibly from the fifties. But it worked and added to the charm. She had a gadget on her phone so she could take credit cards.

The last thing to do was write a slogan on the chalkboard behind the counter. She'd grabbed it from her room before she'd left home, a childhood keepsake from her grandmother on her dad's side.

After a moment's thought, she wrote *Memories Worth Keeping*. Yes. That was perfect.

She checked her watch. "*Seven-thirty sharp,*" Miss Bethany told her, adding that one should always arrive thirty minutes before their shop opened. Watching the second hand, at the stroke of eight, she flipped her sign from CLOSED to OPEN and waited, her legs shaking beneath her, at the counter.

Fifteen minutes later, her shop was still empty, but then the little bell rang, and she looked up expectantly. It was Lexie.

"Hi, Holly!"

"Hi there, Lexie. Love the snowflake pajamas."

"Thanks. Daddy sent me over. I'm here to help with your first crowd."

Holly glanced around the store. "I don't see a crowd yet, but...hey. We dream big, right?" She high-fived Lexie. "Especially since I've invested every last nickel into the place." There was no hiding the desperation in her voice or how widely she was trying to stretch her smile.

"Oh, they'll come. Have faith. That's what Mom

always used to say."

Holly glanced at Lexie. She had wondered where the mother of these spritely children was. "Where is your mom, Lexie?"

"She died a few years ago."

"Oh, sorry to hear that."

"She would have loved this store."

"Well, I bet your dad is busy over there, huh?"

"Gladys, Dad, and Eli are handing out Christmas goodies in front." She leaned in. "Dad's wearing snowman pajamas, and I'm not even kidding. He usually sticks with the moose."

"Ah."

Suddenly the bell rang, and the door opened. Her first customer! But right as she was about to pop off her stool and scramble toward the nice-looking woman, Lexie grabbed her arm.

"Not yet…steady…wait for it," Lexie whispered.

"What am I waiting for?"

"Play it cool. Don't pounce."

"I feel like I should pounce."

"Watch and learn." Lexie smiled at the lady. "Welcome to Holly's Hobbies, otherwise known as Deck the Hollies during Christmas!" Lexie grabbed a flier and held it up to read. "Our first scrapbook party will be tomorrow night."

The woman smiled warmly and took the flier.

Holly grinned at Lexie. "You're good."

"And look! More customers!"

A couple trailed in.

"Yeah," Lexie said like she was an old pro. "You can't be all car salesman like. Trust the system. They will buy. Just be friendly."

"Got it. Thanks. I come from a more...high pressure environment."

"This is such a neat idea," Lexie said. "I've seen stores that sell this stuff before, but not ones that host parties. I want to make a book for Dad for Christmas. Use some of our family photos, so I can remember Mom."

Holly smiled. What a sweet girl. "You can have whatever supplies you want, payment for being my helper."

"Coolio." She played with a paperclip while Holly kept an eye on the customers. "What made you move to Bethany?"

"I needed a change."

"Won't you miss your family? Especially for Christmas? I assume you got the loud memo that all of us need to be open for the holidays."

"I'm right where I want to be."

"You won't be sad without them?"

Holly glanced at Lexie. She looked like she was brimming with at least ten more questions. "Let's just say I need a break."

"Do you have a mom?"

"Yes, a cranky one, with an equally cranky dad.

I can't say they like each other all that much."

"Are they still married?"

"If you can call it that, yes."

"If I had a choice, no matter how cranky, I would never be away. Definitely not for Christmas."

Holly smiled, but deep down she knew she hadn't had a choice. For her own sanity and well-being, she'd had to leave them all behind.

Chapter Ten

With her hands clasped behind her back, Miss Bethany strolled the sidewalks of the town, inspecting everything and greeting townspeople and visitors alike. Oh, the joy that filled the streets. Her own joy, though, was distant, like memories she couldn't quite reach, flickering through her mind.

Still, she waved and greeted. Waved and greeted.

While Willow ran errands for her, Miss Bethany took some time to stop by Deck the Hollies. The sign looked beautiful, as she'd suspected it would. Inside, she saw Holly with customers, greeting them and helping them. She stepped toward the glass for a better view.

She watched until the two customers came out, then hurried herself down the sidewalk. But she didn't get ten steps before she heard, "Miss Bethany, wait. Wait. Miss Bethany?"

She took a deep breath and turned on her heel.

"Yes, Holly. What is it?"

"What do you think? Is it okay?"

Miss Bethany glanced over her shoulder, toward the store. "Thank you."

Thank you? What did that mean? Miss Bethany continued to walk, but Holly trailed her.

"Miss Bethany, so the name of this town. Are you named after it?"

"It's named for my ancestors who founded it. Go tend to your—"

"I've always wondered that."

Miss Bethany paused. "You said you'd been here before."

Holly nodded, then pulled a locket from under her shirt, holding it up for her. Miss Bethany could hardly believe her eyes. She looked up at Holly. "You're that little girl?"

The young woman's eyes glistened, brightly reflecting the light. Now she saw it, now she saw her as a little girl. How could she have missed it?

"May I see?" Miss Bethany asked.

Holly opened the locket for her. Miss Bethany peered closer. There she was, nearly twenty years ago, and there Holly was too. Miss Bethany put a finger on their tiny faces.

"I gave this to you when we buried that little box." She pointed toward the B&B...or was it the Toy Store where they had buried it?

"I never forgot about you, Miss Bethany. And

what you tried to do."

"Tried?" Miss Bethany huffed. "I didn't try, I did it!"

Holly laughed. "I know. My parents listened to you while they were here that Christmas." She let the locket slide back into her shirt. "It just didn't stick."

"And that's why you're back now." Miss Bethany looked toward the shop again, feeling her own eyes water, though for years she'd been able to will back emotion with sheer determination. She smoothed out her dress, then her tightly wound bun, and got herself back into proper shape. "This store, it's as if you brought a piece of Lily's heart back into town, Holly. I'll be forever grateful. Now, if I'm not mistaken, I think you have a customer waiting for you. Or at the very least, a handsome young man next door."

Liam stood on the steps of his porch looking toward the hobby store, as he tended to do in the very recent days, Miss Bethany noticed.

"Oh, I better go!" Holly patted her on the arm, and Miss Bethany let her. She despised the pat. It had started when she'd begun to age, people patting her like she was a pet, but Holly's touch seemed natural, and so she only smiled and waved her on her way.

She decided to take a rest. Her body wouldn't go like it used to. She walked to her apartment, still waving and greeting, and climbed the stairs. Inside, she put on some tea and sat in her recliner, thinking of Lily. Perhaps time healed, but the heart grew smaller every day, now that she had less to fill it.

She'd barely had time to drink her tea and rest her feet when she heard a noise at her door, a knock, and then someone calling her name. Grumbling beneath her breath, she got herself out of the recliner—not an easy feat—and made her way to the door, which she'd kept chain-locked ever since she'd turned sixty.

"Miss Bethany? It's me, Holly. Are you in there?"

Miss Bethany opened the door. "What is it, dear? I was just resting for a bit. Who is looking over your store?"

A mess of confusion passed over her face. "Um, well, we're closed now. Because of the tree lighting. It's about to start, and Willow said we don't start without our town matriarch."

Miss Bethany opened her mouth, but then paused. She glanced toward the window. Though the blinds were closed, she knew immediately there was no sun to keep out. It was pitch black outside.

"What should I—?"

Miss Bethany shut the door, keeping Holly outside, hurried to grab her coat, looked into the mirror once to make sure she was, indeed, dressed and fixed. Yes, she had changed into her evening dress. But when? She unlatched the door.

"Why didn't you say so?" she said to Holly. "Now, let's make haste and get there."

She shut the door, noticing Holly was trying to glimpse inside. Snoopy girl. She shooed her down the steps.

As she stepped into the night air, she heard the carolers: *Silent night, holy night. All is calm, all is bright...*

Holly left her side and joined Liam and the kids. Willow was jazzing up the tunes with a tambourine now, and everyone was singing *Jingle Bells*. Miss Bethany made her way to the front, onto the small podium used to elevate her so the crowd could see.

Willow cut the last refrain of *Jingle Bells* and handed the microphone to Miss Bethany. She looked into the sea of people, some she'd known for decades, others newcomers. The familiar faces were becoming less and less familiar, some dying off, at least she thought that's what was happening.

"Miss Bethany?" Willow said.

"Yes. Yes, I'm..." She straightened up and put the mic to her mouth. "I know many of you have joined us for decades for the traditional tree lighting. We thank every one of you. Sherriff, take it away."

"Countdown please!" Sheriff Jackson said.

The crowd yelled the numbers from ten down. Then the tree lit up. The people clapped and cheered. Miss Bethany, though, could not do more

than stare into the night and wonder where all that
time had gone.

Chapter Eleven

"Thanks, Holly!" Lexie clutched the bag of paper and scrapbooking supplies. "Don't tell Dad, okay? It's a surprise."

"Lips are sealed," Holly said, zipping her lips closed. She'd come to really like this little girl over the last few days. Last night at the tree lighting ceremony, this little one sung *Away in a Manger* at the top of her lungs, like Jesus was standing right in front of her.

Lexie grinned and rushed outside. It was about time to close the shop and get ready for the scrapbooking party later. She stared out the window, looking at the magnificent pine glowing with Christmas lights. What a feeling of community. What joy this place brought! Still, there was a lingering sadness that dulled the shininess here.

She'd called Kinsey earlier, letting her know she was still okay. She called during the school day when she could leave a message and not have to have a detailed conversation with her. Everyone else she left alone, even though her mother and father continued to call, leaving messages laced with the theme of disappointment. *How could you just leave us like that, Holliston? Do you not care at all about what we're going through?*

Her parents seemed to be the only two people on earth who insisted on calling her Holliston. Everyone knew she preferred Holly. Her parents just didn't care.

A ruckus outside had her pausing in her work. She stepped to the window and heard heated words, but she couldn't see anything from her vantage point. Didn't seem like this was a place where fights broke out, so she cracked open the door to see what was going on.

Miss Bethany stood in front of Oscar's store, hands on her hips. Holly couldn't see her face, but she could see Oscar's. His expression was hard to read, because it was all bunched up.

"You know by now, Oscar, you can't get away with not having decorations! Get your Christmas spirit and get it *now*!"

"Is that a rule?" He pretend-scratched his head. "I plum forget."

"Selective memory, eh?" Miss Bethany threw a gesture into the air.

"Now, you listen to me, Miss Olive Bethany. I have put up with you —"

"Put up with me! You're lucky I haven't revoked your lease for insubordination! I don't know what I've been thinking!"

Tourists strolled by. Gladys and Ernie, walking back from the Snack Shack, stopped and watched near Holly's store, munching on their newly purchased popcorn like it was the matinee.

"Oh, just write me up, woman! I'll add it to the pile. I could make me a scrapbook of them at Holly's store." He pitched a thumb toward Holly. It made her cringe. She just wanted to be a bystander.

Ernie cupped his hands together and shouted at them. "Would you two pipe down to a dull screech?" He looked at Holly. "It's a thing with them."

Gladys decided to jump in. "Ooh, tonight's feature is *spicy*..."

"No one could remember all of your rules and mandates. *Regulates*. You'd think you were writing canon code!" Oscar said.

"War of the Stinkin' Roses," Ernie said to Gladys.

"How long have they been like this?" Holly asked over Miss Bethany's heated response. It brought no sense of entertainment for her...just memories of her parents fighting over the smallest of things, like wallpaper color, and big things, like hours spent at work.

"As long as I can remember," Gladys said. "It's

gotten worse over the last two years or so." She shrugged. "They always get over it. I think they make up so they can start the whole thing over again."

"Oscar!" Miss Bethany screeched. "I'm not gonna tell you again!"

"Well, goo—ood. Color my ears tickled!"

Miss Bethany stomped off. Oscar threw his arms up, but he didn't seem as mad as his fighting words indicated. He stopped, turned around again, and called after Miss Bethany. "Does that leaky faucet still need fixing at the Welcome Center?"

"Yes!" she yelled back.

"Fine then! I'll be over tomorrow!"

"Fine!"

And they parted ways.

"Show's over," Gladys said.

"See what we mean?" Ernie said with a wink.

The crowd dispersed, but Holly just stood there, wondering if it worked out for anyone, anyone at all. Maybe Ernie and Gladys. Yes. And Annalise and Christopher seemed happy, though Annalise had mentioned that they'd been unable to have children. The pain in this life...sometimes it was too much to bear.

"I feel like hot chocolate could fix it."

Holly looked up, startled to find Liam standing in front of her, hands in his pockets.

"What?"

"Hot chocolate. It sort of fixes anything, and you seem like you need something fixed."

"It's coming through right here, isn't it." She circled her face with her finger.

"Like a beacon." He took her shoulder and guided her toward the B&B. "Come on. I know just the thing."

Minutes later, she sat on a soft carpet in front of a roaring fireplace, in a small sitting area nestled to the right of the entryway. Nearby, a Christmas tree twinkled like a bright evening sky. A few guests came and went, merriment in all their voices. Behind her, Lexie and Eli were asleep on the couch. Liam covered them with blankets, then brought her a mug of hot chocolate, topped with whipped cream.

"All the festivities have worn them out. I can't remember the last time they've fallen asleep before seven." He nodded toward her cup. "We make this double Dutch hot chocolate from scratch, by the way," he said, and joined her on the carpet. "So...where were we?"

Holly glanced at him. "I was on the sidewalk, and you offered me hot chocolate."

"Oh yes. And you were ruminating over something unhappy." He offered a kind smile.

"My parents. They...they don't believe in me. That I can do anything outside of their world. Maybe my dad was right. A month ago, I had a healthy savings account, a well-paying, secure-for-the-rest-of-my-life job."

"A month ago, it sounds like you couldn't breathe."

A couple, newlyweds it seemed, came through the front door, giggling all the way up the stairs and to their room.

Holly stared into the fire. "I wish we could go back to what it was like that time here. I didn't realize then that Lily was the daughter Miss Bethany had lost. Miss Bethany just focused on putting my family back together."

Liam nodded. "She does have this way of making sure anyone who comes into this town broken somehow leaves fixed. And half the time, they don't even know she's doing it. Between her and Chris and Annalise, they have saved many marriages. If I sense I have a pair of guests in trouble, I get them on the case."

"This is the first tourist town I've heard of that saves families and marriages. I've never been a part of something like this, something that felt like it mattered. You guys all seem like a family."

"I don't think I could have survived these past few years without them."

Holly wanted to ask about his wife, what happened to her or how she died, but instead she let the awkward silence hang between them until she thought of a topic shift.

"So Annalise tells me you homeschool the

kids?"

"I try. Sometimes I fail. But I try. And Annalise helps me."

"They are blessed that you want to spend that much time with them."

"And they're still at the age where I've fooled them into thinking I'm fun and maybe even a little cool." Liam stoked the fire with a poker that had a reindeer on the end. "To be honest, I wasn't always like this for them. There was a time I barely knew them. Worked long hours. It was my wife, Heather, who pushed for a change. Encouraged us to move here, starting a business where we could homeschool them."

"What happened to Heather?"

"We'd been here a year. Pancreatic cancer. A few weeks after she was diagnosed, she was gone."

"I'm so sorry, Liam."

"Sometimes I wonder if she were inspired, you know, in some kind of divine way, to set all of this up before she left. I'm sure she thought she'd be part of it." He set the poker down and looked into Holly's eyes. "Last year, I promised my kids it would just be them and me for awhile." He looked like he was trying to find the right words. "I had met someone over a year ago. She runs an inn in the next town over. Grove Hill. They got really attached to her. But in the end, she said she always sort of felt like I was looking for a mother for my kids, not a wife. She made me realize how not-ready I was to start over."

Holly nodded, appreciating the honesty, and looked away, because his eyes were so intense and...gorgeous. They sipped their hot chocolate while Liam shared more history of the town.

She sat back and enjoyed the stories.

He set his mug on the coffee table. "You're doing a great job over there, by the way. It fits you like a glove."

She smiled. "Thank you. That means a lot. And speaking of, I've got a scrapbooking party to get to."

"You late partier, you."

"Yeah. Really, it's a club. So I'm going clubbing."

Liam laughed and helped her off the floor, pulled her up like she weighed nothing more than a dandelion.

"Thank you for this amazing hot chocolate." She took a small step away from him and let go of his hand.

"You're welcome," he said, and she turned, feeling a blush set in, because he was that gentleman that she always thought didn't really exist. And here he was, "not-ready." But then again, neither was she.

* * *

Thirty minutes later, the ladies had arrived at her shop. They sat on either side of a long table in the back, chatting happily as they cut shapes, passed stickers and organized photographs. Annalise introduced another resident, Jayden, who brought her baby Jaylee, asleep in her carrier as Annalise rocked her with her foot. Just then Lexie arrived, carrying scrapbooking supplies in her arms.

"Ladies."

"Lexie?" Holly said. "I thought you were asleep!"

"Just a nap. I wouldn't miss this." She sat down next to Holly, then held up a picture of her mother for everyone to see.

Gladys put a hand over her heart. "Your daddy is gonna love that."

"It's a surprise for Christmas. Also, Daddy doesn't know I'm here, so…"

Holly laughed. "Lexie…"

"It's fine. He's busy with inventory. He'll never know I'm gone. And yes, Anna, all my homework is done."

"Good girl," Annalise said.

Lexie got down to business and was picking out just the right stickers when Miss Bethany walked in. Surprise swept the room, hardly hidden by the murmuring.

"You got any of those journal papers to put notes by photos?" she asked.

"Sure do." Holly hopped up to help her to the table and get the paper off the shelf. Miss Bethany put a box down on the table and sat next to Gladys, who apparently had no idea how to hide surprise.

Holly cleared her throat, hoping to indicate everyone should get back to their business. "You want flowers? Blank? Themed for a holiday?" Holly asked.

"Blank." Then she paused. "No. Wait. Every holiday. Deduct the cost to the money you owe the city for your business license."

Holly looked down for a moment. Miss Bethany knew bills were tight. What a kind thing for her to do. She grabbed several pages and delivered them to Miss Bethany, who looked oblivious to the shock everyone was doing a poor job of covering up.

When Holly returned to her spot and sat in front of her own photos, she noticed hers looked kind of old compared to everyone else's...except Miss Bethany's.

"What are you working on there, Holly?" Gladys asked.

"Just an old family vacation."

Miss Bethany looked up and gave her a weak smile.

Lexie leaned over. "You don't have anything new to scrapbook?"

"Hasn't been much worth photographing before I came back here."

"That's unacceptable," the little girl said. "We need to change that."

Gladys was stamping pages. "Holly, you leave behind a hunka-hunka boyfriend back where you came from?"

"If he were hunka-hunka, do you think she'd be here by herself?" Miss Bethany said with the kind of sideways glance only Miss Bethany could give.

"*Boyfriend* is not what I would call him."

"Ahhh!" Gladys looked like she might bust with excitement. "What's the scoop? We like us a good scoop,"

"There is no scoop," Holly said. For the first time, Lexie looked up from what she was doing, stared at her without blinking.

Little Jaylee, the baby, fussed, and Annalise signaled to Jayden she would get her. She lifted the child, bouncing her in her arms, and said, "All I have to say is you want to make the right choice on the front end."

Jayden threw a hand in the air, yelled, "Amen!" Holly noticed she didn't have a ring on.

Lexie pitched a thumb toward Annalise. "Take her word for it. She knows what she's talking about. She and Christo-Pop really like each other."

"They have the fairy tale we all wish we could have." Gladys smirked. A couple of gasps came and went. "Oh please. You all know I love Ernie. It's just he gets on the last of what few nerves I have left."

Annalise shrugged shyly. "Well, listen, it's not like life has gone according to our plans." She looked down at Jaylee, smoothed the top of her head. "But we've gotten through those ups and downs together."

Lexie was happily snipping paper and without even looking up asked, "Miss Bethany, you think about getting married again?"

Uncomfortable glances went around the table, to which Lexie was oblivious. But everyone looked over at Miss Bethany, expectantly as a groom waits for his bride to walk down the aisle.

Miss Bethany hardly missed a beat. "And who on God's green and precious earth would I marry?"

That brought a round of silent snickers and ornery winks, but then everyone went about their scrapbooking without another word about it.

An hour later, Miss Bethany was the first to turn in. She gathered her things and said her goodnights, reminding everyone of the events coming up on the calendar. Holly helped her to the door with her box and project.

Just outside the shop, Holly said, "Miss Bethany, I hope you'll come to our next hobby night."

"Oh, you bet I will. I have a big project to finish."

"Thanks for, well, putting these toward my bill. Sorry about that. I don't think I really knew what I was getting into with start-up costs. The whole cash flow thing."

Miss Bethany took the box from Holly.

"I can carry these up for you," Holly said.

"No, thank you. And you're very welcome. I'm really glad you're here." She turned toward her apartment, hesitating just a bit, Holly noticed, at which direction she should go.

"Me, too, Miss Bethany," Holly said.

"Good night, dear Lily."

Chapter Twelve

On the porch outside the bed and breakfast, Liam handed out little wrapped baggies of biscuits and bacon, the only part of the breakfast they were able to salvage. For grits and eggs, he was pointing them toward the diner. Holly joined him as she wiped the flour off her cheek. She'd been summoned by Lexie, who said there was an emergency. Upon arrival, she found that Gladys had pulled a hamstring that morning, and Liam was on his own to make breakfast for the guests.

Flour covered the counters and a whole carton of eggs lay splattered across the floor. It was hard not to roar with laughter, but she knew this poor guy was desperate for help, so she went straight to work.

Together, biscuits and bacon was all they'd managed.

Liam smiled at her as she stepped next to him. "So that whole clean eating thing…?"

"A ruse. I had a nanny."

He laughed.

She eyed him. "The man who runs the bed and breakfast doesn't know much about breakfast."

"I know how to eat it."

Down the sidewalk, Oscar was suddenly up in arms, grumbling so loud they could hear it from where they stood.

"Uh oh…" Liam groaned.

"What's the matter with him?"

"Early this morning Miss Bethany came by and *hired* the kids to do some dirty work for her."

"What kind of dirty work?"

"Oscar still hasn't put up Christmas decorations. So she hired them to paint the nativity scene on his store front window before he got there."

"Yikes. Looks like he's not taking it well."

They both leaned out to get a better look. He was flailing his arms, raising his voice. Lexie and Eli looked pinned against the window.

"Should you go help them?" Holly asked.

"They'll be fine. We have this scenario, in one form or another, every year. The kids are just usually a little more covert about whatever they're hired for." Liam handed a biscuit to the young newlyweds as they passed by. "Good morning! Sleep well?"

They nodded enthusiastically and went on.

"Anyway, so…Lexie has it in her head that you need some picture ops. She said your collection was…dismal. Her words, not mine."

Holly grimaced. "That bad, eh?"

"She wanted me to invite you to our annual tradition, a hike up the mountain to find snow. Would you like to join us? I promise a lot of work and sore muscles."

"That is so kind of her." And it was. Holly appreciated the invite, but she couldn't shake off the feeling that she shouldn't go. He'd told her of the disastrous relationship he'd gotten out of. It was too complicated, especially since the invitation didn't come from him. "I think I better just stay with my store and—"

Just then Oscar shouted something about getting the sheriff and making an arrest. She looked at Liam.

He seemed unconcerned, his focus still on her.

She bit her bottom lip. He was a man who confessed he wasn't ready for any kind of relationship. Now he was inviting her hiking with his family?

Willow was rushing by, looking determined to get somewhere quick.

"You! Willow! Stop right there!" Oscar limped toward her, his gait half the strength of his mouth.

Willow sighed, turned around, saw Holly and Liam, and gave a forlorn look before directing her attention toward Oscar. "Yes, Oscar?"

"Where is Miss Bethany? I demand to see her.

The sheriff said he can't arrest children, and they're vandalizing my property!" He looked at Liam. "I'll get into it with you later, B and B." He pointed his finger back at Willow. "Where is she? Up in her apartment?"

"Miss Bethany went out of town for the day. I saw her head for the parking lot out back."

Oscar's hand dropped to his side. "Our Miss Bethany? Impossible. No. She never leaves here. Never during this season especially." He glanced at Liam and Holly. "You two hiding her in there?"

Liam shook his head. "No, sir."

"Your two pipsqueaks are covered in flour, by the way," Oscar grumbled. "What? Did they vandalize a kitchen too?"

"No, um, that was—"

"I want to speak to her now. Right now," Oscar said, pointing to the sidewalk to make his point.

Willow lowered her voice. "The thing is, Mr. Oscar, she's been escaping."

"Escaping?" Oscar unclenched his fist.

"Every Wednesday, for the past while. When I try to ask why, she gets all defensive-like. She won't discuss it with me."

For the first time since she'd met the man, Oscar looked soft as a teddy bear. "You think she's okay?" he asked Willow.

"I don't know," Willow said. "If you'll excuse me."

Willow continued down the sidewalk, leaving Oscar to think for a moment, unaware of their watchful eyes. When he turned, he noticed them again. "Liam, you're a moron."

Liam raised an eyebrow. "Is that so?"

"There you are, holding biscuits and bacon on your porch, oblivious to the fact that you're standing under mistletoe with a pretty girl by your side." Oscar stomped off.

They both looked up, and Holly clutched her heart, taking a long, sideways step to the right. Liam laughed.

"You would've thought you were standing under a viper's nest," he said.

"Right. Well, I better get to my shop."

He held up a sack. "Bacon to go?"

"I cannot pass up bacon."

"It's on your clean eating diet?"

"It is."

"Holly," he said, "will you think about the hike? It would mean a lot to...Lexie. To the three of us. To me. She's, uh, never asked for anyone to go on the hike before except the three of us."

"I'll think about it. Thank you for the invitation. It was very sweet of Lexie."

He smiled. "See you later."

As she took the short walk to her shop, she considered the invitation. Was it from Liam or Lexie? And why did it matter?

She also couldn't help feeling worried for Miss Bethany. She hadn't been here long, but she knew something...*something*...was amiss.

* * *

Though she ate alone for every meal she took in her apartment, Miss Bethany always thought it proper to sit at the table for her meals, with a napkin in her lap, with the television turned off. There was no other place to eat a meal than a table, as far as she was concerned. Certainly not on a *T.V. tray*. Certainly not out of a sack.

She was happily slicing in her scrambled eggs, firm like she enjoyed them, when a horrible racket rattled her door, such a racket that she dropped her fork, which flipped her bacon onto the table.

She raised her eyes to the ceiling, asking for strength, for perhaps one of the fruits of the spirit to carry her through this moment. Because there was only one man in this town who didn't know how to knock in a civilized manner.

"Not home!" Miss Bethany picked up her fork and her slice of bacon.

"Come on, woman! I know you're in there!"

"Am not."

But she knew...oh how she knew...how persistent Oscar was, how he wouldn't let a single thing go until it was his idea. Perhaps she should let him in now, allow him to vent his frustrations—she was certain it was over the nativity scene—and get on with her day. She had a lot to do.

She shuffled to the door while he continued to bang the everlasting daylight out that wood. She finally opened it, freezing his hand in mid-air.

"Where were you?"

She returned to her breakfast.

He trailed behind her.

"Oscar," she said, her voice calm. She knew the calmer she was, the calmer he'd be. It always worked that way. If she brought her voice down to a whisper, so would he. "First, I'm eating. Second, you need to let the kids finish that half-done nativity scene."

"Where were you?" he repeated, more softly, as predicted.

"What good is a nativity with just two shepherds, no wise men, and a missing Jesus? Do you want to be responsible for a missing Jesus?"

"Woman, are you deaf...?" But he stopped what was sure to be a rambling diatribe and eyed her plate suddenly.

Miss Bethany noticed but went on about her eating. "I had business. Out of town."

Oscar crossed his arms, but his voice was much softer now. "Your business is this town, woman."

She set her fork down and turned to him. "You don't know everything about me, Mr. Oscar

Menlow."

"That may be true, but I do know you never, ever eat breakfast in the evenings."

Miss Bethany looked at her plate. Had she done it again? No, not again. She'd made sure, hadn't she? She'd made sure it was the right time.

Oscar's hands were now on his hips. "You got you an out-of-town boyfriend?"

Miss Bethany rose, taking her unfinished eggs and bacon to the sink, quickly washing it down. "Right. That's it. Mystery solved."

"You would tell me, right?" He stood at the small breakfast bar and leaned on it with both hands.

She turned away. "I don't have to tell you anything. Now, you need to get on your way. I've got a lot to…" She peered out the window. Only her reflection peered back. "Well, you just need to leave."

"I came over to see…"

She turned to him, because he didn't seem to be able to finish his sentence. He seemed stricken by a particular emotion she couldn't identify.

"Yes? What is it, Oscar. I don't have all morning, er, evening."

"I came over to see if you wanted to take our annual drive through the area. To see the Christmas lights."

"You hate doing that." Miss Bethany scrubbed

her plate.

"I know it. But you don't like driving after dark."

She set her plate down and studied his face, the one she'd watched grow into an old man over three decades.

"Fine. Let me grab my sweater. I'll meet you downstairs."

"Fine."

Oscar left, not before reminding her to get her glasses too. After he'd shut the door, she stood a long while at the kitchen sink, wondering how much time would slip away.

Tears stung her eyes, but then she marched to her bedroom and grabbed her sweater. Nonsense, all this blubbering. It was what it was. She would go see the Christmas lights. She loved them. It was a tradition, after all, and tradition was what kept it all strong, kept it all going, kept her going.

And how kind of Oscar to remember for her.

Downstairs, Oscar had the car waiting, already warmed and cozy. She hardly needed the sweater. She looked down and saw he even had a travel mug full of Liam's hot chocolate waiting for her. With marshmallows.

"Thank you for the marshmallows."

"The small ones, like you enjoy."

"Yes."

For a while they drove. He played the

Christmas songs on the radio, the old ones that were her favorite—and his, she suspected. They passed the festively lit up streets, where every home participated. Lighted arches shone over every intersection. Some homes even had speakers playing Christmas carols. Other homes had themes. Still others glowed bright with white lights. They were all beautiful to her. All of them.

Oscar turned the corner onto her favorite street. "What is it you love so much about this time of year?"

Miss Bethany thought for a moment, then decided to answer, because Oscar's question, she could tell, was a genuine one. "It changes people. Makes hearts all soft-like. For a short season, people are generous. Caring. Not in a hurry."

"You're always in a hurry, woman. Especially this time of year."

"I'm in a hurry, Oscar, so other people don't have to be. Also, you do know I have a name and it's not 'woman.'" She gazed at a beautiful mountain home lined in white and red lights, with enormous pine wreaths and red bows on every window. "Our visitors over the years, well, they don't leave the same after spending Christmas with us." She couldn't help the heavy tears that must've been visible in her eyes. "All of those families we've saved…"

"I wish yours could have been saved, Miss

Olive Bethany."

"Me, too. Me, too." She patted his thick, meaty hand. "But I've been blessed with the family our town has become for one another." She glanced at him as he glanced right back at her. "I couldn't have made it without you."

Oscar's eyes grew big at that moment, and his grumpy old face turned as tender as the first flowers poking up from the soil in the spring.

Miss Bethany looked ahead. "Watch the road."

Chapter Thirteen

After a great deal of thought, Holly decided to go on the hike. She wanted to know these trails, and shouldn't go the first time by herself. Also, Lexie dropped by and begged her the way only a ten-year-old can.

She wasn't entirely sure she was dressed appropriately for a hike. She'd never imagined she'd be hiking with a great looking guy and a couple of adorable kids when she hightailed it out of town and fled here. But fortunately she did bring some decent boots and a pretty warm selection of sweaters. They'd loaned her some gloves. And now here she stood, at the bottom of a trail, ready to begin.

Lexie held up a digital camera, which, she'd informed Holly, had been a gift the previous Christmas. "I'm going to take a thousand photos, Holly, so we can make nine scrapbooks."

"Nine?" She elbowed Lexie in the ribs. "Not twelve?"

"If you insist."

Lexie and Eli laughed and raced up the trail and out of sight.

Liam handed her a stick.

"You might have to carry me off this mountain," Holly said.

They headed up the trail, a good hour before there were screams of delight: "Snow! Snow!"

Liam hurried ahead, but Holly took her time. The view was so gorgeous and the conversation had been so fulfilling. Liam and the people in Bethany cared about what mattered in life.

She'd never taken the time, never made the commitment to come to parts of the country where these kinds of things existed — the people, the view, the spirit of kindness and community. The air was so crisp and clean, the kind that holds the lungs full for far longer than it has to.

All that worry and heaviness she'd brought with her, like another stuffed-to-the-gills suitcase, melted away.

She caught up to Liam as he was warning the kids to watch for ice. They were rolling and tumbling and throwing snow, little balls of energy, their voices echoing off the cliff walls.

She watched for a little while, envious of the energy these two had. And even as her cares of the other life melted, the ones of this new life edged in. Her little shop wasn't doing as well as she'd hoped.

She wasn't daddy's little, obedient girl anymore. If this failed, she was certain her father would not be there to bail her out. Or if he did, it would come with conditions.

She caught Liam observing her. "That's an awfully big frown for such a little lady," he said.

She cracked a smile. "Sorry. No frowning allowed up here. I saw the sign."

"It's okay to frown."

"I'm thinking of my shop. I'm just not sure if it was such a good idea for a store. People are so used to doing online diaries now. Thankfully, Gladys is going to let me pay her in supplies for watching the store today. Otherwise, I couldn't afford to pay her."

He nodded silently, deep in thought. Finally, "You're offering something completely different. It's not just a store, and it's not just for photo albums. You're offering community. Not just for tourists, but the rest of the women in town. And believe me, that's a good thing. Sometimes we get so caught up with the tourists that we forget we have each other." He stepped next to her and turned to watch the children. "Give it time."

"I don't know how much time I have. I invested everything into that store. I don't have much to live on."

"Well, don't give up too soon. Our biggest weekend is coming up. And hey, breakfast is on me every morning, okay? Come by for some of *Gladys's* cooking."

Then a snowball hit his face. Holly laughed and stepped out of the way. She took her phone out and snapped a photo of the snowball fight, which she managed to stay out of, probably because Liam warned the kids ahead of time not to pound her. But she did make snow angels with them as Liam took pictures.

Then Lexie grabbed her hand. "Let's take a picture together!"

She pulled Holly into a hug, and they both gave thumbs up as Liam snapped the photo. Holly was having so much fun, she hardly noticed when Lexie slipped away. She realized she was gone and had an instant of fear, then spotted her at a lookout. Liam was building snow castles with Eli, so Holly joined her.

She nudged Lexie in the arm. "Hey, what are you doing over here all by yourself? There's a lot of snow architecture going on back there."

Lexie looked out over the valley, her cheeks flushed bright pink. "Sometimes I'm afraid I'll forget Mom." She brushed pieces of hair out of her face. "Sometimes I'm afraid I'll never forget her."

Holly put a careful hand on her back.

"She died when I was seven. Already I am forgetting her voice."

"She'll always be in your heart, though."

Lexie nodded. "But if she's in my heart...is

there room for someone else in there too?" Lexie looked at her, her eyes twice as big trying to hold in the tears.

Holly wasn't sure what Lexie was getting at, but she couldn't help but wonder if she meant her. And this was the exact thing that Liam had said he didn't want to happen to Lexie...again.

"Well, Lexie, I've never lost my mom like you," Holly said. "And I'm not a mom myself. But I think in most cases, moms want their kids to be happy. They want their families to be happy. They want them to be safe and have everything they need. If I were a mom, that is what I would want."

"Even if you weren't there anymore?"

"Yes. Even if I were not there." She paused, wanting to make sure she expressed herself in the right way. "You, Eli, your dad...the three of you have everything you need to be happy."

Lexie smiled. "Okay then." She checked her watch. "Come on! More pictures! We haven't even reached two hundred yet!"

Lexie ran and Holly took one more long look over the valley, breathing in the air. Oh how she wished she could say that about her mom. Wasn't a mom's instinct to make her children happy? Why didn't hers have that instinct?

When she turned, she found Liam nearby, watching her, smiling at her. And then he snapped a picture.

The sun was dropping toward the western horizon. It was time to go. As they made their way back down the trail, the kids rushed ahead.

"So your dad's company, it would erase history?" Liam asked. He'd asked about her leaving it, and Holly was doing her best to explain.

"You could call it that. I hated it. It's like all his clients wanted was to forget the past, bury it, crisscross shred it. Some of those, sure, they were legit, like safety from identity theft, but sometimes, what clients would pay…I always felt like we were covering up things that shouldn't be hidden. But it paid big. And Mom got used to her high society life, spending everything Dad earned."

"And you didn't want to work there for the rest of your life?"

Holly shook her head. "No. It was like working with people who were everything I didn't want to be…living lives worth forgetting."

The rest of the walk, Holly asked about Liam's wife, who she was, what she was like. She asked about the town, about Miss Bethany, and by the time they hit the bottom, she felt like she'd earned her citizen's degree.

Back in the town's square, it was getting past dinnertime. Liam took the kids to the diner, but Holly wanted to check on her store, which Gladys had locked up at five. But even before she unlocked the door, she could tell someone was in there. A single light was on.

She was savvy enough now to know that the chances of her shop being burglarized were close to nil, but she still wanted to investigate.

When she unlocked the door and walked in, there sat Miss Bethany, alone at the scrapbook table, feverishly working. Paper, tape, glue, stickers, scissors, and photos were strewn all around her.

"Miss Bethany?"

The old woman didn't even flinch, quiet and alone with her thoughts. Holly didn't want to startle her. She took a careful step forward.

"Miss Bethany?"

"Oh, hi dear." She still didn't look up.

"How's it coming?"

"I have to finish," was all she said.

"Can I help?" She flipped on a few more lights.

"This is something I need to do." She stole a glance at her. "I wouldn't mind if you wanted to work on something for yourself. Beside me."

"Sure. I'd appreciate sitting down. Climbing that mountain was hard work." Two mountains, actually—the hike and the idea that although she was drawn to Liam, she had to keep herself from getting attached.

"I'm really thankful you're safe." Miss Bethany gazed at her for a moment, but at something else, really, something beyond the room, then went back to her scrapbook.

Holly turned to gather her things, yet she couldn't help the nagging feeling of that last sentence...said in such seriousness, so somberly.

Next to Miss Bethany, she set her scrapbook down, opened it quietly. She wanted to ask Miss Bethany if she was okay, but instead they just worked side-by-side, all the way past dinner and late into the night.

Chapter Fourteen

Church. It was not something her family put much stock in, aside from Easter and Christmas, where they attended stoically, like they'd arrived for military duty rather than worship. She never saw her father grimmer than when he attended church services, so she did not have warm fuzzy feelings about church, except when she'd attended the week they stayed in Bethany when she was a child. This church held a different atmosphere. Light flooded through the windows. Joy filled the spirits of the parishioners.

And though the preacher had changed, the air was still charged with everything she imagined church was supposed to be.

Christopher was now the preacher—voluntary, Liam explained, though they took an offering up every once in awhile for him. He often assured everyone he'd do it for free, and the folks suspected he took that love offering and gave it away, since soon after, somebody around town would suddenly get their mechanics fee paid for, or their plumbing fixed for nothing.

It was a good sermon. Christopher reminded the folks that God gives promises long before he fulfills them, to give his people hope. He read the story of Abraham and Sarah, who had to wait twenty-five years for better days to come, but those days came.

"No matter what you're facing, no matter how difficult, joy comes in the morning. We may not know which morning, but it will come."

Christopher's words still hung inside Holly's heart long after church was over. She stood near the stage, having watched the church members bring the costumes out for the nativity play. Each was laid upon the stage for inspection, and everyone was doing a job. Except Holly. She was the odd man out, but she didn't feel like it, because so many people smiled at her when they passed.

Annalise and Christopher were dressed as Mary and Joseph. She laughed watching Sheriff Jackson and Liam talking sports while in their wise men costumes. She even noticed Oscar, of all people, dressed as a shepherd, though he didn't look happy about it.

And then, appearing suddenly like the angel she was dressed as, Lexie gave her a sweet, sideways hug. "We need to find you a costume."

"Oh, uh, well, no..." Holly chuckled nervously, the kind that seems polite but is really screaming *no*. "I'm perfectly fine watching."

Her darkest secret was that she'd fainted in fourth grade. She'd played a carrot in the school play and had one line. *I'm a favorite snack of horses.* She got out, "I'm a...horse..." before falling into the arms of Chuey Martinez, who smelled like steak year round.

Like Lexie had read her mind, she turned toward her father, who was on the stage. "How about she plays one of those lowing cattle? What does *lowing* even mean?"

"It's a prolonged moo," he said, descending the stairs toward them.

Lexie put her hands on her hips, elbowing her wings out of the way. "Did you just make that up?"

Eli followed his father. "Dad," he whined. "You said we were having real cows this year." He turned. The entire backside of his pants was ripped. Annalise, all the way from the stage, lifted her eyebrows, then grabbed the to-do list she'd been working, no doubt adding *fix Eli's costume.*

"I said they were *thinking* about it."

"Why not say the cattle are *mooing*?" Lexie asked.

"Hard to rhyme," Willow said, hurrying by.

Miss Bethany took center stage, clapping her hands loudly. The noise settled.

"Everything this year," she said, her voice

carrying the entire length of the church, "has to be perfect!"

Miss Bethany continued on, but Holly was distracted when, very quietly, Oscar slid up next Lexie.

"Have you figured out yet why Miss Bethany leaves town on Wednesdays? And where she goes?"

Lexie eyed him. "You're late on your payment."

"I've got powdered donuts waiting for you at the store."

"Fine then. I've not gotten all the details, but I'm working on it. I'll get you the information as soon as I get it."

"Very well," Oscar said. "And permission granted to finish the nativity scene on my window."

Lexie glanced at him. "Yeah?"

He nodded and slipped away.

The entire Sunday was spent working on the nativity play, the costumes, the props, and anything else that needed to get finished.

As the evening drew to a close, most had to leave to tend to their families, but Annalise and Willow were still there, sewing away. Holly wasn't very good at sewing (or singing, they informed her, when she was told she *couldn't* participate with the choir because she couldn't hit C minor), but she could cut fabric, it turned out.

She glanced up at Annalise. "Would you mind sharing with me what happened to Miss Bethany's

family? No one really talks about it around here."
Even Liam had not raised the subject during their
hike.

Annalise nodded a bit. "It's not a secret, it's just
that everyone here knows already so it's not talked
about much. And Miss Bethany still suffers from a
lot of grief. Her daughter, Lily, wanted to go hiking
one day in search of snow. It's a tradition around
here, if you don't already know." She gave Holly a
knowing smile. "Here in Georgia, sometimes we
have to go up some elevation to find it. Lily talked
her dad into going, but not Miss Bethany. They
traipsed off together, like they often did. But they
never came home. There was an accident, some ice."

Holly sighed, realizing what Miss Bethany's
words had meant the other night when she seemed
so relieved Holly had made it home from the hike.
"How did you and Christopher end up here?"

Annalise's whole face brightened. "We got
married nineteen years ago."

"You don't look old enough." Holly said.

"God bless you." She grinned. "Anyway, our
families are on the west coast. But we both felt we
should move. All we heard from God was 'go east.'
So we went. It was the two of us and whatever
would fit in our VW Rabbit...which wasn't much."

"You didn't even know where?"

"Not until we landed here. We felt like we
should take over the diner. It was called Mel's at the

time. The owner was getting old. Miss Bethany...she saw something in us. We had no money to invest, but she helped us get started. And then four years after that, my husband began preaching at the church, at first part time. Then he became the full-time preacher, when he's not flipping burgers." She laughed and shook her head.

Annalise continued to share their struggle to have children and how this town had helped them heal, how they became like parents to many who came and went, and to those who stayed. They didn't know if they would have children, but they were happily invested in those whose paths crossed theirs.

Holly cut fabric until she could hardly think straight. She needed to stretch her back, so she took a walk to the rear of the church and looked out the window.

She spotted Liam and Sheriff Jackson on ladders, hanging a banner across Main Street. It read *It's a Victorian Christmas.*

Holly smiled. Maybe for them. But for her, it was more like *A Victorious Christmas.* This was what she always wanted but never knew she could have.

If only this store would take off. And, if only that handsome, wonderful man on the ladder had a piece of his heart to give her. He'd made it clear very early on that he was not ready to be in any sort of relationship. Most likely, neither was she. She'd run—more like bolted—from a man that everyone told her was right. It took her months to unchain herself from Noah and have the courage to say so. It took one look around her home, void of pictures, to tell her it was the right thing to do. She pulled her phone from her pocket and tapped her messages app. She typed a simple note to her mom and dad.

I am fine. I am not coming home for Christmas.

Her finger hovered over the send button, but instead, she erased the message and slipped the phone back in her pocket.

Chapter Fifteen

When Holly stood in this store and helped customers, it felt like *home*. She couldn't explain the truth behind it—she knew she was lucky to have grown up so privileged. But privilege, she now understood—and perhaps always knew—didn't make a home.

She wanted to stay open later tonight, as other shops did, to take advantage of their final big weekend of the Christmas season. There was bustling of people outside, just like in the city, but the spirit was different. There was joy. Excitement. Energy of a different sort.

She watched the people outside. They clearly had their favorite stores, pointing and hurrying to this store or that. Would she be one of their favorites? In due time?

An hour passed, and a few people had come and gone. A young brunette, around thirty, was now perusing the shelves. Every time a customer walked through the door, Holly felt pure giddiness, restraining herself (like Lexie had taught her) from jumping up and down. Instead she simply offered a warm smile and help if they needed it.

A while later, the young woman's basket was full, and she made her way to the cash register. "You better get me out of here before I blow through all my cash," she said.

Holly laughed. "Is this a gift?"

"One set is for me and one is for my mom. She'll love doing these."

Holly got a gift sack out and put one set inside it. "Well, if you ever come back through town, check out our Hobby Night schedule and join us."

The woman paused and touched a nearby basket of stickers. "My mom and I haven't always gotten along, so this is...a peace offering. She loves photo albums, and this is something we can do together. It's perfect."

She wondered how many lumps-in-the-throat Miss Bethany had to fight every time a family was touched in some way by her town.

"I'm glad to hear that," Holly said.

It took a good five minutes to compose herself. Luckily the store was empty for the time being. What an impact she could make with this store. What if it grew just a little bit more, became a staple of the town? People would tell their friends. Maybe word would spread.

The little bell rang again with a new customer. Holly blotted a tiny tear from her cheek and turned with a smile. It fell right off her face like lead to the floor.

"Mom? Dad?"

They stood at the entrance, blocking the door with their bodies and their displeasure. They looked dressed for a high society dinner, not a quaint little town. Her mother stared at her. Her father was glancing around the place as if deciding whether it held the plague or not.

"What are you doing here?" The words wheezed out of her mouth.

Her mother straightened a collar that was already starched perfectly in place. "Funny, Daughter. I was going to ask you that."

Her father stepped ahead and placed his hands at his waist, almost like he was expecting a cape and super powers to arrive. "So, you *do* remember who we are. I was expecting to find that you'd had an accident. Bumped your head. Suffering from amnesia. What good child doesn't let her parents know where she is?"

What good child...?

She blinked away the tears, held onto the counter in front of her for whatever support it would give.

"I'm not one of your clients who wants to forget the past."

By the fluttering of emotions that passed over his expression, she knew that stung.

Her dad's arms dropped to his side. "Why did you run away?"

That was a genuine question. For the first time she saw real pain in his face.

"Dad, I ran *to* something. It's not the same thing." She stepped from behind the counter, but held onto it nevertheless. "I'm glad to see you both."

They stood there like neither knew what to do, so she walked to them, gave them each a hug, though hugs had always been awkward in her family. Productivity, not warmth, was the theme.

Her mother was now flailing her arms like she did when she was upset and couldn't do more than talk about it. "Well! If you hadn't left your tower pinging cell phone on, we wouldn't have been able to find you." She gestured toward the window. "Deck the Hollies?"

"Holly's Hobbies in the off season. Cute, isn't it?"

"Looks like child's play to me," her dad said, his voice growing low as it did when he wanted to assert his authority. "Did you forget you have a life? A career back home?"

"And you have a fiancé!" Her mother waved her hand in the air like Noah might be hanging from the ceiling. "Who, by the way, you left the night of your engagement party. Poor man. Do you have any idea how humiliating that was? For him? For us! You come home this instant!"

"My fiancé—" But that was all that came out, because the little bell rang, a customer entered, and her parents were gracious enough to step aside. Liam strolled in, but apparently hit the wall of tension and tiptoed back out, slinking away. *Great.*

"Sorry," Holly said, returning to her register. "I know how important your reputation is."

"Your business"—her father cast an abhorrent glare toward the craft table—"is it thriving?"

She tried to stand taller, but she felt like a little kid. "I'm working on it." She looked him in the eye. "It is new. Even you know these things take time."

"So then, no. That's your answer. Where did you get the money for this?"

"My savings."

"You blew your life savings on this?" her mother asked, mouth gaping open. Perhaps she was surprised that it wasn't on a fur coat or a vacation cruiser.

"I wouldn't put it that way." Holly kept her tone as even as possible.

"What if it doesn't succeed?" her father asked.

"Maybe it will fail," Holly said. "But at least here, I'm allowed to try. Your business almost failed many times, and now you're one of the top in your industry."

Again, a sweeping glimpse into her father's

soul…a man who had many fears, who had many failures, who couldn't admit to one of them.

"Holliston," he said, his voice the softest she'd ever heard it, "I have built my life around it. To ensure you would be taken care of for the rest of your life. My company…it's both of yours. Yours and Noah's."

"I don't want it." She hated how it came out, but it was the best truth she could communicate. "I've never wanted it."

She regretted the words immediately. Hurt flashed through his eyes. His hands clasped the bottom of his sweater because they had nothing else to hold on to.

Her mother put her nose in the air. "I'm sorry, Holliston, but we need you to come home."

"Why?"

They glanced at each other, then looked back at her. Neither said a word.

"I need to close up for a few minutes. I promised I'd go visit my friends in the nativity. You are welcome to join me."

They didn't move.

Suddenly Willow poked her head in. Her eyes were perpetually wide, like she was always expecting catastrophe, but they looked especially wide now.

"Willow? Everything okay?"

She nodded politely toward her parents,

believing, Holly was sure, they were just ordinary visitors to the town.

"Welcome to Bethany. Um, have you seen Miss Bethany?"

"I haven't today. I'm sorry."

"She's probably just in a corner somewhere, giving Oscar the..." But her voice trailed off, and she slipped out without another word.

"Yes, welcome," Holly said, and squeezed between them. "Join us if you'd like. Or not."

Holly walked out, inching between a food cart and an ornament stand, both of which her parents were sure to turn their nose up at.

Chapter Sixteen

It was hard to believe her whole life fit into this suitcase and a few boxes, but the truth of the matter, Miss Bethany knew, was that her whole life was this town, and it wasn't hers to keep. Not really. It was hers for a while, to watch over, to cultivate, to bring in the harvest when it was ready. But it was not hers to keep as her own.

Her apartment was bare now, except for the red bucket they drew names from. Yes, that she would leave. That was tradition. Her photographs, her favorite sweater and other personal items, she'd taken one at a time for weeks now or donated to the nearby shelter. All that she had left was in the suitcase.

This apartment, with the window overlooking the town, was a haven. It had given her a feeling she couldn't put into words. It was a warm blanket for her soul on the darkest and loneliest of nights. But it couldn't keep her safe any longer. It couldn't fix her.

It would serve well the next person to oversee the town.

She managed her way down the stairs, clunky as she was, until she got to the bottom and exited out the back door into the alley. She stepped to the side, to look one more time, to say goodbye.

She took pride that she'd left it in order. Her town was a well-oiled machine, but a machine with a heart, and the heart was all the people who saw what it could do paired with all the people it could help. It was alive and breathing, its own self-propelling mechanism if the spirit was kept alive as it should be. And indeed it could be with people like Christopher and Annalise, with Willow, hard worker that she was, and Ernie and Gladys. Holly, the dear heart. She had great expectations for that girl.

Even Oscar…yes, Oscar. He was not the calloused old soul he wanted everyone to believe. She would miss him the most. Perhaps that would surprise people if they ever found out. Her gruffness was matched only by his. Oh, those wonderful times when they would go toe-to-toe. Yes, she would miss those, even if she couldn't remember them.

A noise caught her attention—it was a noise she was not used to hearing apart from herself: discord. She put her suitcase down and peeked around the corner of the alley. Holly was leaving her shop, trailed by two adults who looked stuffed straight into their coats.

Her parents. She recognized them, the mother's nose in the air, the father's march-like walk.

Miss Bethany held onto the wall and watched, marveling at how she could lose a whole day but remember a face from twenty years ago.

She could barely hear them, but they were talking, waving their arms. Holly stopped, turned, said something back and kept walking.

No...no, no Miss Bethany. You must go. This is the time you've planned, the busy Victorian Weekend. Nobody will see you go. Nobody will try to stop you. You are to slip out and be gone, just like that.

She'd lost a daughter. Even so, she was still a mama, and mamas had bears inside of them, ferocious ones when their cubs were in danger.

Holly had made such strides since she'd been here, come into her own, as they say. *It can't be undone by two selfish, short-sighted parents.*

"Not on my watch." She moved her suitcase behind a trash bin. "Not on my watch."

* * *

Holly could barely comprehend it, but it was happening. She could tell by the onlookers, trying to look away but not able to. Her parents were following her, practically yelling their protests.

Finally she pulled them to the other side of a

light post.

"The only people allowed to yell in this town are Miss Bethany and Oscar. It's a peaceful town. It's festive, see? Jolly? Good will and all that?"

"Every town has its secrets," her mother growled. "Don't be so naïve."

"Holliston," her father said, pointing a finger at her, "you should live up to what you promised."

"I never promised! Noah never asked me to marry him. Did you know that? No knee. No question. Just a box shoved across a desk at me. He just assumed I would say yes. All of you did. Is that really the kind of man you want for me?" Tears streamed down her cheeks.

"You have to come home," her mother said, ignoring the question, the very heart of the matter. "Or your dad could lose everything."

"What are you talking about?" Holly asked.

Her father sighed, and it seemed his anger slipped away. She saw another glimpse of his fear. "It was always understood that Noah would eventually own the company. With you. When I retire. He's fighting now for breach of contract because of you."

"In his view," her mother added, "if you were married, he'd technically own it all one day. Noah is holding your father to it."

"Our lawyer says he has a case to at least keep half or more, or we'll spend a lot of money fighting him." Her dad looked as dejected as she'd ever seen him.

"Then give him half," Holly said. "I may not agree with what he's doing to you, but you know he deserves a cut with or without me. He brought your company into this century when he designed Control X." She swiped away a final tear. "You know, I'm a lot more concerned about the idea you want me to marry a man I don't love, who I've never loved, so you can save your company. What? Does Mom just not want to give up her spending allowance?"

"Don't talk to your mother like that," her father said. Though his words lacked conviction.

"Why not?" Holly asked. "You do! I've heard it my whole life. You guys ruined any chance we ever had to be a real family with all your sniping and complaining. I don't want your life. And I don't want your marriage. What I do want you can't give me. Better memories is what I want. You can't fix that now. And I'm sure you don't even want to, because that would take effort. You can't hire it out."

Mean words. So mean. But they came spilling out so fast, so hard, that the three of them were breathing as hard as if they'd just run up that mountain.

And then, like she'd stepped out of the shadows, Miss Bethany was by her side. "I thought we settled this years ago," she said to them.

"Daughters like her…they are wasted on people like you."

Her parents' eyes widened, like they'd been stabbed with the knife of truth. Her mother's bottom lip trembled. Her father was the very definition of aghast.

Miss Bethany looked perfectly calm as she slipped her arm around Holly's waist. "Holly, don't ever stop living the life you know you were meant to live. I mean it. Promise me. Now."

Holly touched her locket and grabbed Miss Bethany's hand. "I promise, Miss Bethany."

Then Miss Bethany turned back to Holly's parents, who seemed like small children against the older woman's pointy finger, directed right at them. "I had high hopes for you, that you'd wake up in time." She turned to face Holly. "I can trust you, Holly. You're going to do just fine here. Your store, it's exactly what we needed to build community. You are what I needed."

She kissed Holly on the cheek, stared down her parents, and turned to march toward the Welcome Center.

But Holly couldn't shake the feeling that she'd just been told goodbye.

Chapter Seventeen

𝒜 day and a half later, in the middle of the night, as cold as it was, Holly knelt on the back lawn of the B&B. It didn't seem she'd been found out, though she wouldn't have minded the presence of the warmest man she'd ever met. She of course had never known and would never meet Lexie and Eli's mom, but by the way the children's faces lit up when they talked about her, she knew in the short seven years she'd been in their lives, she'd made an everlasting impact.

Holly knew she'd always wanted to be a good mom. The note was already in her box. Her own mother never knew how, but she knew how, and the truth was by missing the mark so diligently, her own mother had taught Holly what not to be, and how to make sure she did it right.

But now there was a new note: BE A GOOD WIFE. It was written on a small piece of scrapbooking paper.

She closed the lid and placed the box in the ground. With only her hands, she covered the hole with the dirt she'd dug up shortly after she'd arrived in this town. Liam had never even had the kids fill the hole. She patted it down nicely and then quietly walked the lawn back to her home.

But she was still restless, even at two a.m.

Instead of tossing and turning, she decided to walk down to her store. But she was drawn to the front door of her shop. The warm, twinkly lights of the town surely could be seen from heaven. If asked her opinion, she'd say Bethany was practically its own slice of heaven, right here on earth.

As Holly stood there, she noticed lights on at Miss Bethany's apartment.

Was she home?

Miss Bethany had disappeared sometime during the early morning yesterday, or maybe the night before. Nobody could find her, but Holly was the last one to see her, the night of the nativity play. Her car was gone. Her belongings were gone. They gathered at the church to pray for her. Sheriff Jackson said they couldn't file a missing person report, since it was clear she'd left on her own accord. They knew that when they saw her clean — and empty — apartment. She clearly didn't want to be found.

It baffled everyone, but the overwhelming feeling was a sweeping sadness.

Now, though, her lights were on. Was she back?

Holly couldn't help herself. She hurried to Miss Bethany's apartment, raced up the stairs, and didn't even have to knock. The door was open.

Sitting at the table was not Miss Bethany. It was Oscar, slumped over some file folders, his face grim.

"Oscar?"

He jerked upright, looking right at Holly, a brooding indignation shadowy across his face.

"What are you doing here?" he grumbled.

"I...I saw the lights on. I thought Miss...I thought she came home."

"She's not coming home. She's never coming home."

"Where is she, Oscar?"

Oscar pushed the file folders toward her. Holly sat down at the table and gathered them, glancing through each one. "I...I don't understand." Each folder had names written on them: Christopher and Annalise. Oscar. Ernie and Gladys. Liam. Willow.

And Holly.

Inside Chris's and Annalise's folder were deeds to the diner and the church property, now stamped *Paid in Full*. And *transfer of ownership from Olive Bethany to Christopher and Annalise Goodwin"* had been written there.

Oscar's folder contained a *paid in full* note too. So did Ernie's Toy Store. And Liam's Whistlestop Bed and Breakfast.

She looked up at Oscar, who only watched, stoic and silent.

Then there was her folder.

Inside was a note that read, "Holly, I believe in you." And behind it, documents confirming her store and apartment were now hers.

The rush of emotions that overtook her didn't seem to surprise Oscar, who looked away out of courtesy, perhaps, as her tears spilled to the table.

"What...I don't understand, Oscar. What is this?"

"She had them mailed to me. They arrived yesterday. Miss Bethany," he said, "is giving us the town."

Oscar sighed deeply, a small, warm smile, rare for him, covering up what seemed to be bigger, louder emotions. "She signed over our places to us. No rent. No future payments. We own them now." He slid another folder toward her. "She's putting you and Willow in charge of managing the rest of the shops that are still rented."

"Me? But...?"

"Didn't you hear her?" Oscar's voice was gruff but his eyes were soft. "She believes in you. And when Miss Olive Bethany believes in something or someone, then it's official. They're worthy. You're worthy, Holly."

Holly wiped her tears. "Why would she do this? Is she okay?"

Oscar traced a finger over the folder that held his name. "Some will say she's out of her right mind. She's never been one to relinquish control. But I've known Miss Bethany a long time, and she does nothing by accident. All this...it's no mistake."

"But...why would she leave before...It's almost Christmas." Holly caught his mournful eyes. "Oscar, you know where she is, don't you?"

"She doesn't want any of us to know. For years I've always been her *in case of emergency* contact on every form she's ever filled out. And she didn't even want me to know."

There was something in the way he'd said it, the *didn't* in the sentence that made Holly think he knew more than he let on.

"But you know, don't you, Oscar?" Holly said carefully and gently. She put a hand on his. "What are you waiting for? You go get her. You must. She belongs here, with us."

Oscar looked distraught for a moment, but then he grinned, as wide as the North Pole is from the south.

"Yes. I know."

* * *

Miss Bethany rose with the sun to get her room in perfect order. Everything was tidy now. Not warm. Not comfortable. But things were in their place, as they should be. No Christmas tree. No decorations. That was a season in her life...a long, wonderful one...but it was over now. For now it would only remind her of what she had to leave behind. Before long, she would forget about it anyway, and her days and nights would all be the same. If the Good Lord were willing, she would go soon, but the doctor had told her the bad news...her body was in perfectly good shape.

There was a knock at her door, and then the kindly attendant...Marci? Megan?...came in. "Miss Bethany, you have a visitor."

Miss Bethany gripped the arm rests of her chair. "I have a visitor? Impossible. Nobody knows I'm here."

"Santa knows."

"Oh...no, I don't want to see the man dressed up as Santa. Thank you."

"It's not really Santa. He just said, 'Tell her Santa Claus is here to see her.'"

"I'm confused."

"Then he said, 'She'll know.' Then I said, 'Is she expecting you, Mr. Claus?' and he said, 'There ain't nothin' about today she's gonna expect.' He doesn't have the trademark beard...but he does have a twinkle in his eye."

Miss Bethany was taught never to open her mouth in surprise. Her mother taught her, and it had been passed down from her grandmother. The

Bethany women were never to "swallow flies" as her grandmother put it. But here she was, mouth agape.

"Then, um," the attendant continued, "he said to tell you that he's not going anywhere until you show your face in the lobby, and that he will make a scene, hollering your name and—"

"I'll be there," Miss Bethany said. "In one moment."

The attendant left and Miss Bethany rose. She straightened her sweater, adjusted her necklace, and pinched her cheeks.

Chapter Eighteen

As the sun rose, Holly swept the sidewalk in front of her shop, but her mind was hardly on the task. She was overwhelmed with the gift that Miss Bethany had given her...*gifts, so many she could hardly count*...and she was mindful to spend her life wisely, carefully, and in full service to others, just as Miss Bethany had.

Her parents had abruptly left town, but she'd hardly thought about it. It was easier with them gone. She couldn't deal with them *and* this all at the same time. She'd have to try to make it right with them at some point, but she didn't have it in her yet.

A shadow passed over her, and she looked up. Liam stood there, grinning like...well, like it was Christmas morning. She set her broom aside. She'd been worried about Liam too, whatever he might've accidentally heard her say to her parents when he'd stepped into the shop as they were discussing her engagement.

"Liam, hey. I'm so sorry, it's been so crazy around here. I've been meaning to stop by and, um, well...I don't know what you heard, but—"

"It's okay. You probably don't know this, but your parents landed on my doorstep last night. They stayed at the B&B."

"They, uh...they did? I thought you didn't have vacancies."

"I didn't. We brought them to the guest house. You should know, I did not iron the sheets."

Holly laughed. "That was brave of you."

Liam shuffled his feet a bit. "Um, so...are you, I mean...?"

"Engaged? No. Never have been."

Liam smiled. "I'm so glad to hear that." He then pitched a thumb toward the diner. "By the way, your parents are already up and grabbing breakfast."

"At the diner? Impossible. They don't eat diner food."

Liam just gave her a knowing look, gently touched her arm, then walked back to the bed and breakfast. Holly checked her watch. It wasn't near time to open. She hurried across the street to the diner. If her parents were eating biscuits and gravy, she was definitely going to be snapping a picture.

Inside, she found them in a corner booth. No biscuits and gravy, but hash browns and omelets covered their plates...big helpings of each. She laughed just as her dad looked up. He waved her over, a smile on his face.

She grabbed a chair and joined them. It seemed nobody knew what to say, so Holly decided she might as well just jump in.

"So. I'm setting up roots here. Thanks to Miss Bethany, the woman who owns...owned this town...I own my store now." She glanced between them. "She believes in me. She's giving me a chance. I can make a difference here, with the locals and the tourists. When people leave this town, they're different, changed...in a good way."

Her mother set her fork down. "We arrived back in town last night. All the stores were closed, but there was such a warm feeling, all the lights. The spirit here is..." Her mother looked away for a moment, swallowed as if she'd just taken a big bite. "You know, last night, that little girl...Lexie? Yes, Lexie. When her dad went back into the main house to take care of something for a guest, she gave us a sneak peak of that Christmas present she's been making for her dad, at your store."

"Oh? I haven't even seen it yet."

"Well...you're the star of it."

"What? I thought...I thought she was making one of her mother."

"It started that way...but it ends with you." Her mother reached a hand toward her. "Holly, you've made a difference in that young girl's life. And those photos she took of you...I've never seen you look like that, with such life in you."

Holly swiped at tears rolling down her face. Had her mother ever talked so gently to her?

Her father pushed his plate aside. "Why wasn't Noah that to you? What was so wrong with him?"

"With him, I didn't want to take any photos." It was the only way she could explain it. Her father didn't appear to understand, but seemed to accept it.

"Holly?" her mother asked. "Do you mind if we spend Christmas with you?"

Those few words were the nicest she'd ever heard come from her mouth.

* * *

Across the manicured lawn of the assisted living center, decorated with faded wooden Christmas characters chipped over the years and lights that blinked out of unison, Oscar and Miss Bethany walked.

"What are you doing here, Olive?" Oscar asked.

"It was time to move it along."

"Don't give me that," Oscar spat. "You never lived nowhere except Bethany and you ain't gonna start now."

Miss Bethany eyed him. "Since when did you become my real estate broker?"

"Since I spent the past forty some years of my

life doing what you asked!"

"Rewriting history, eh? You've never done what I asked."

"I do sometimes," he said, dropping his gaze like a small child.

"I must have fallen asleep on those days, because I sure as blazes don't remember." She smiled at her own irony.

But Oscar wasn't smiling. He watched her as they walked. "Woman, are you sick?" She didn't answer. She'd not yet said it aloud. "Well? What is it? Cancer? Heart? Lungs? Auto-immune something or other?"

"No, Oscar."

"Then what?"

She stopped then and turned to him. They faced each other right in front of Rudolph, with his little red nose hardly shining bright. "By next year," she said, "I probably won't remember it's Christmas. Just like what happened to Mamma."

It broke right then and there, Oscar's heart. She saw it as clear as day, dribbling down his face, getting into whiskers he hadn't yet trimmed this morning.

"Bethee..." He took her hand.

"You haven't called me that in a couple hundred new moons."

"You remember."

"For now."

"Alzheimer's?"

"Something like that."

Oscar wiped his tears with a hanky. "Why wouldn't you tell us? Why would you come here?"

"How did you find me, anyhow?"

"I put Lexie on the task. For powdered donuts, she did what she does best, snooped around and spied." His thumb stroked the back of her hand. "If not for that, you would've disappeared straight out of this world...out of our world."

"I'm sorry."

"You shouldn't be carrying heavy stuff alone."

"It won't be long before I'll need round-the-clock care. And I don't want to be a burden." The last thing she ever wanted in the world was to be a burden. "Of all the Bethany women, I'm going to die an old maid. I don't have family to take care of me there."

"Now, what kind of harebrained thought is that? What do you think we are?" Oscar took her hands, rubbed his thumbs on the top of her knuckles. "Bethee, if I weren't so sad right now, I'd be mad. You're not stayin' and that's final."

"Bull feathers."

"This ain't a negotiation. I'm writing the ordinances now. You're moving in with me."

Miss Bethany gazed at the ground. "Now, Oscar, I'm too old and too traditional to be shacking up."

"Then I'll make an honest woman outta ya."

There it went again, her jaw as slack and uncouth as most of the teenagers she'd met.

"Oh come now. Don't pretend you haven't wanted this for at least one hundred of them moons," Oscar said.

"Oscar...I'd drive you crazier than a bat in daylight. Or did you forget?"

"Oh, I remember. I've been there."

"Then why would you want to marry me?"

"Because...I'd be more nuts to not have you around driving me plum out of my mind."

She smiled at him. "Well, that's a heap of romance."

"You betcha."

"You know I'll never agree to this unless you promise to put up a Christmas tree."

"Okay."

"Every year."

"Fine."

"And decorate your store window without me asking."

"Anything else?"

She touched his shoulder softly. "I want you to remind me it's Christmas."

"Even if it's Easter?" He grinned.

That got him a little smack across the arm, and then a sweet kiss on the cheek.

Chapter Nineteen

And so the little town of Bethany closed one chapter and began a new one. Oscar and Miss Bethany were married in the old church, surrounded by their friends—their family—on Christmas Eve. Holly knew that what was special about this town flowed from its matriarch, much deeper than the rules and regulations, but straight from her heart, which she gave away to Oscar. It was perhaps the last time she would give it away, but she'd certainly given it to many people over the years. And all those people lined the streets the day she returned, clapping for her as if there were a parade. Oscar drove slowly so that she could see every one of them, young and old, cheering and waving at her, blowing her kisses. Holly was among them, and when Miss Bethany saw her, a tear streamed down her cheek. Holly touched her locket, and Miss Bethany smiled.

Christmas morning was spent fireside with Liam, Lexie, and Eli—and her parents, too—all in their pajamas, warmed less by the fire and more by each other. Her mother fixed a breakfast casserole. Holly didn't even know her mother knew how to cook, but she said it was passed down from her great-grandmother.

And then, with great pomp and circumstance (a snowman dance that Lexie and Eli rehearsed fifteen minutes beforehand), Lexie presented Holly the album she'd been working on so hard.

Page after page was filled with what could only be described as the best memories of Holly's life. She enjoyed every bit of it, laughed at each picture and the little captions below. But she couldn't help the tears, so when the attention was diverted, she walked to the back window of the bed and breakfast and looked out over the lawn, covered with a light snow. From there, she could see the small mound of dirt where she'd buried her box.

Little arms wrapped around her waist. She looked down to find Lexie.

"Don't cry!" Lexie said.

"They're happy tears, I promise. Thank you so much for the album."

"Well, I have to tell you something."

"Yes?"

"My dad, Eli, and I made a deal with each other awhile back for it to 'just be us' for awhile. It was for our own protection."

Holly nodded. "I understand."

"We want you to break it."

"You do?"

"We had a vote last night. Everyone agreed." She took Holly's hand. "I'll never forget Mom. But I'm okay with us moving on as a family."

"I'll take it from here, kiddo." Liam stood behind them, sent a wink to Lexie, who gave a not-so-subtle wink back, not to mention a kissy face.

Holly laughed. Liam took her hands, looked out at the mound of dirt. "I was...I was thinking that, um, well...maybe...I'll change my name to Ken."

Holly shook her head, suppressing a laugh. "Really? That's what you wanted to tell me?"

"Worst pickup line ever?"

"Pretty bad."

"Okay. How about this? My family and I, well, we'd like to build milestones and new and peaceful memories with you."

"I'd like that. Very much."

"May I kiss you?" Liam asked, stepping closer.

"You may."

And there was no mistletoe needed, then or ever again.

About the Authors

Rene Gutteridge is the award-winning and best-selling author of twenty-four multi-genre novels and is a seasoned collaborator in both fiction and film. She has novelized six screenplays and movies, including, *Old Fashioned,* with writer/director Rik Swartzwelder. Her romantic comedy with screenwriter Cheryl McKay, *Never the Bride,* won the Carol Award in 2010 for Best Women's Fiction. Her new titles include two more novelizations with Cheryl McKay, *Love's a Stage* and *O Little Town of Bethany.* Her seven suspense books include *Possession, Misery Loves Company, Ghost Writer* and *Escapement.* Her indie film, the comedy *SKID,* was deadCenter Film Festival's Best Oklahoma Feature Film Winner in 2015 and also won Best Oklahoma Feature at Red Dirt and Trail Dance. She is a creative consultant on *Boo,* a script based on her beloved novel series, which is in development at Sodium 11 Entertainment with Andrea Nasfell (*Moms' Night Out*) as screenwriter. Her novel *My Life as a Doormat* was adapted into a Hallmark film called *Love's Complicated* which premiered in January of 2016 and scored 2.1 million viewers. She is the head writer for *The Skit Guys.* Find her on Facebook and Twitter or at her website:
www.renegutteridge.com

Cheryl McKay has been professionally writing since 1997. Tommy Nelson served as her first publisher, teaming her with Frank Peretti on the *Wild and Wacky, Totally True Bible Stories* series. Cheryl wrote the screenplay adaptation of *The Ultimate Gift*, the feature film starring Academy Award Nominees James Garner and Abigail Breslin. It's based on Jim Stovall's best-selling novel. The film was released by Fox in theaters in Spring 2007 and has won such awards as the Crystal Heart Award, the Crystal Dove, one of the Top Ten Family Movies at MovieGuide Awards, and a CAMIE Award. She also wrote the DVD for *Gigi: God's Little Princess*, another book adaptation based on the book by Sheila Walsh, and episodes of *Superbook*. After being commissioned to write a feature script, *Greetings from the Flipside*, for Art Within, Rene Gutteridge and McKay released it as a novel through B&H Publishing in October 2013. McKay's screenplay, *Never the Bride*, was adapted into a novel by Gutteridge and was released by Waterbrook Press in June 2009. The film version is in development. As one passionate for those who are losing hope in their wait to find love, she released the nonfiction version, *Finally the Bride: Finding Hope While Waiting*. She also penned her autobiography, *Finally Fearless: Journey from Panic to Peace*. She wrote the screen story for *The Ultimate Life*, the sequel to *The Ultimate Gift*.

McKay co-wrote the films, *Extraordinary* and *Indivisible*, both faith-based features. Find her on Facebook, Twitter, Pinterest, or at her websites:

www.purplepenworks.com

www.finallyone.com

www.dateswithGod.com

Dear Readers:

Thank you for spending this time with us. As I (Cheryl) first started thinking through this story, I thought of my grandmother who soldiered on through the loss of her husband, my grandfather, early on in life. She heroically continued to raise five kids without him. She also began to lose her memory many years before she passed away. Yet, she'd have these amazing moments of clarity just when we needed it. She gave me some of my best childhood memories.

We hope you were blessed by reading this story and inspired, like Holly, to live a life worth capturing in photographs. Having family members who are losing their memories is sadly common today. Sometimes, we need a reminder to treat each day as the treasure it is. So, now that you're done reading, go out and make some good memories.

If you enjoyed this book, please recommend it to your friends and family. Would you mind leaving a review online where you purchased this book to share your thoughts with others? Thank you kindly.

Blessings,

Rene Gutteridge & Cheryl McKay

Books by the Authors